THE GREY

IAN MACKENZIE JEFFERS

Inquiries concerning rights should be addressed to:

William Morris Endeavor Entertainment, LLC
1325 Avenue of the Americas
New York, New York 10019
Attn: Kathleen Nishimoto

ISBN: 1614190283
ISBN 13: 9781614190288

Thanks to Eric Simonoff, Kirby Kim, Gordon Lish and George Andreou, all of whom helped make this book possible.

For my wife, and our children, and our life together.

1

FOUR WEEKS ON, four weeks off. When you're off, you sit in a bar in Anchorage, stare at the bottles, sleep in a motel, if you don't have a house, and bit by bit you soak away whatever you made when you were on. When you're on it's easier, you're already numb from the cold at the bottom of your blood. It comes from the ground up, from the air in, step by step, breath by breath. Inside, everything's over-heated, the food hall, the bar, the game lounge. Everybody steams. You come in from a shift and ice melts off you, drops in your dinner tray or in your drink, if that's your dinner. I found the only camp on the North Slope with a bar. When you're determined you can do anything.

Oil comes out of the frozen shale and two thousand of us watch it flow, pump it through. I sit in a shack with a rifle and stare at the snow, shoot the occasional bear if he thinks a cook is going to fight him for a bag of trash. Some of the guys make friends of each other. They have families, save money, call home. These are not bad guys, but I don't make myself one of them. I make myself the least of them. I don't call home. I watch the snow, make myself invisible. If I've learned anything from animals, it's that.

The food hall's the size of a hangar. Vats of pre-fab eggs and every other pre-fab thing, pool tables and foosball tables and cigarette machines. We have a hoosegow, women of loose god-knows who get themselves there somehow, a chapel with a neon cross over the door. We have bull-necked jocks and walking nerve-cases, scrappers, we have beer and scotch and air-wanks and fist-fights, recreational buck-knife parties. We have greater and lesser morons, idiot-crews, guys who go quiet when they bump you at the bar then burst out laughing five feet away. High school jokes, for those who got that far. Some guys say I'm a curse. Shadow of death, a specter of something, what have you. You're too friendly to me you're dead before your shift is out. I don't blame them. Put in the time, six months' dark a year, you get superstitious. Everybody likes to go home alive. Most of us.

We have guys who snap, like anywhere else. They go mad as a dark stairway, up some hall in their head, and don't come back. There are deaths from time to time. Heart attacks, guys walking under trucks, falling into the rat-holes or jumping in, drowning in mud. They always do a service, human resources does, even though the body's going to get flown away somewhere else. I always go, know the guy or not. Sometimes I'm the only one. Sometimes Tlingit is there. I don't know his real name, his mother's half-Tlingit, half-Inuit, or something else. Everyone calls him Tlingit. Some of the Inuit guys go too sometimes, like I do, know the guy or not.

There's a pastor who's a dry drunk. He runs meetings. AA meetings, grief meetings, my wife's fucking the neighbor and I'm six-thousand miles away meetings. He slip-foots around the camp half-spooked, like he's afraid he'll get his hands on a bottle or he's suddenly remembering something he wished he hadn't. But he has a way with an unexpected death and a cargo plane. He'll look at you like you stepped on his crotch if you pass a pint at one of his send-offs, but he won't say anything. Some of us are regulars,

2

after all. 'The Lord is my shepherd,' he says, his nose always running. His eyes too, from cold. Or he has more to cry about than the rest of us.

The chiefs of the idiot-crew, the ones who make jokes in the bar, Lewenden, Bengt and the others, elbow each other if they're passing, if they see you watching the box go up the ramp. As if sending off a dead guy is an idiot thing to do. They know better, by way of smokes and shots and big talk. Banging glasses on tables makes you infinite wise.

"All those guys need is a neck-snapping," Tlingit says, watching them laugh their way by, sucking their cigs, being better than the dead and better than fools who care. I've watched enough coffins flying away it doesn't seem so bad. A bright day, snowy runway, blue sky, waiting. Job-advancement, from the job at the end of the world. No looking back and no need to look further.

My fathers and their fathers moved up here when it was wild Klondike. They rolled up from the worst of the lower states, before that some dark lump of rock in an ocean of bad doings. A tribe of white men too bad and damned to be put up with anywhere else. The sons and grandsons stayed, and with few exceptions did things bad enough to deserve living here and dying here.

They were hunters, man to boy. Not the noble kind. The living things my ass kind. The pay me I'll kill what's bothering you kind. They fed their families, year on year, but they didn't like it all the way, say what they wanted. Not the way they did it. My father hunted for the state, once we became a state. When he wasn't doing that he hunted for anybody's dollar. He was killing animals for their good, he said, which was a lie that affected his outlook. I think it did. I hunted for the state too, until the day I didn't like it either. Then I was going to do all kinds of things. At least there was a moment when other things seemed possible, or that I was winding my way to them. But I got mailed further north instead, by this and that. This and that and no complaining.

My father told me there's a wolf in the heart that makes you do things. "What does it make you do?" I'd ask him. "It depends on the wolf," he'd say.

I look up. Wall of bottles, bartender. Yes please, certainly. Last day, and all that attends your last day. Heading north, four more weeks, four weeks closer. I don't like the down-shift. But you can't stay up there. They make you leave.

And here I sit and wait for the taxi, because there's no staying here, either. Bag's packed at my feet, goodbyes to the digital clock and cinder-blocks and the long hall and guy who doesn't know me at the motel, nothing left behind, as always. Snowplows and buses grind outside, taxi's there, waiting. The wind pounds at the windows, like it hates you, in particular. Drink down, time to go north.

At the airfield I look out the windows, thumping in the wind. I can see the wind shredding lines of snow across the runway like curtains rip-flapping. It's bucking the wings of the planes, scaring the wives and girlfriends come to say goodbye. Bulldozers grind back and forth pushing the runway clear, but it's white again in no time, white slam. The company has a 737, big plane, and it's wobbling, trying to jump off the ground and flip over and die. But they're telling us we're going, it's just bump. I don't want to spend another night down if I don't have to. It was a comfort once to be near people, even people who never wanted to see me. But that faded. The comfort did, not wanting to be near them. Maybe that faded too. Cold takes everything away. You go out on the tarmac and it hits you like knives. It goes through you like you're nothing, like time, something in the universe you've displeased, like the wind at the bar. You'd think they'd have one of those enclosed ramps everybody else has. Not this company.

They wave us over. We're half-running across the tarmac, slipping and sliding. Some stop as long as they can stand it, loved ones say goodbyes, I-love-you's. You see the family guys, worried faces, the what-might-happen looks, weeks away in that terrible place, and I hope all is well while we're apart, I hope we're together again. God knows what happens in an instant when your back's turned. Look at a flock of birds, the one you love is under a bus, go off on a weekend, she's died while you're gone. I see that in their faces, some of them, as I'm trotting my bones, stiff as boards, past hands that cling and part, past kisses, and I feel sorry for them. Which is comical.

I haul up the stairs to the plane. I've been outside forty seconds and my legs are numb, my face. On board, families behind us, heaters hit us. The guys who know each other say their hellos, another four weeks missing their families, bored to death, only each other to look at.

I stay out of this too, though I know most of them, by name at least. Flora and fauna, beasts of the forest. Some of them getting on nod to me. Most don't. Half of them think I'm a parolee. Somebody made a joke I'd been killed in a hunting accident. It went around the camp, somehow it got turned into that, that I killed someone somewhere. I hear the idiots, others too in the food hall, calling me 'Oddway,' more laughing. I don't run around correcting people.

I buckle in, look at the tarmac, watching the snow blow across, waiting to go. This is the shift when night is going to move in and sit down like a dog and refuse to leave. Six months of dark, after the first few days when every day's shorter by an hour until the last one's down to minutes, then dark day and night, permanent fluorescents, shift after shift, through spring. If you haven't gone crazy and jumped in a rat-hole to drown, by then.

There was a night I went out in the snow with my rifle, got a wire tied around my boot and the other end around the trigger, got the muzzle into my mouth. I sat there, wind blowing, and I stared into the tumbling snow in as final a mood as that. I got myself set to yank my boot down on the wire, three deep breaths, and ready, my last seconds, I think, staring into the snow falling and blowing and folding on itself like an ocean. And out of the tumbling comes a big white bear, forming out of the snow, head swaying left to right, sniffing for the dumpsters, or me. When he sees me he rears up high, all of him, black eyes, black nose, three black pennies aimed at me, and a little line of black gums, I thought I saw, a little snarl.

I look at him, with my gun in my mouth, and I get it out and get it turned on him, if you can find any sense in that. I don't think he was afraid of me. I didn't see him getting angry, but things can surprise you. Maybe he never made me out in the snow, but I sat there pointing my gun at him until he dropped on his fours, turned sideways, into snow again. I was afraid of him, certainly.

Sometimes up there you see aurora, purple winking in the sky, red, green-gold. That night I did, sitting on the snow, like a coward, after the bear left. A great green-gold curtain dancing, and it glowed and rippled over me all the way back to camp as I carried my rifle and the wire in my pocket, fool's cargo. For later use, maybe. At a time to be determined. They're the only colors you'll see for months, but you've never seen anything like them on earth. They look impossible, like a lot of things.

I see Henrick getting on the plane. He comes up the aisle, climbs into the seat next to me. He's one of Lewenden's friends, one of the idiot-crew. I see him with them. But he's alright, as much as any of us is. Smarter, maybe. He belts in, nods at me, to say *'You might be the psycho we're all afraid of, but I don't have a beef with you.'* He knows not to bother talking to me, and he doesn't seem to mind. This is what I like about him, partly.

The other heroes file on, Lewenden, Bengt, the others. They look at Henrick sideways, for sitting with me I suppose. But Henrick's the one who'll thump them to shut up when they're laughing their way past a funeral or throwing bottles across the bar. I should like him less for spending his shift with fools, but I like that he sticks to his friends, backwards or not. And they stick to him, I've seen that too. So they're not nothing I suppose. None of us is I suppose, whatever we think. Whatever signs to the contrary.

We're belted in, blathering, bluffing, bullshitting and playing cards, with bags and our laptops and game-boys and phones and shit to read and Playboys and packed lunches and long underwear and teary eyes, some of us, and would-you-fuck-her looks at the company flight-attendants and another four fucking weeks and we're off, as much as the wind is letting us. It's slapping us up and down for thinking we could, right now, and the wings are bucking worse. But we're men of the north, we're better than any wind. The plane hoists, shoves this way and that, humps and bumps but gets up there. We get up over it, like they said we would.

Out of Anchorage a little, not dark yet but I see all the orange lights crawling away below, like stars upside down. We leave it behind and sooner or later we're over dark snow. I watch it pass under us, it gets darker mile by mile, snow and ice, on and on, for-ever. Everything leaks out of it, all the white, the little black lakes get harder to see, until there's nothing to see at all. If you wanted the world gone you could fold it up and bury it here under the snow and never see it again.

We fly on, smooth as sleep. I tick by like the clock, last one awake, same as when I was little. "You're a night animal," my father said. "You'd rather watch than sleep."

But I close my eyes eventually, and I see the motel room, the cinder-blocks, the dresser, the mirror. Weeks in a motel room, you'll start to hate the mirror, at least the guy looking out of it. I see the clock on the nightstand, the picture, half-crumpled, my wife, when she knew me, our boy, when he knew me.

I stare at it, in half-sleep, like I did in the room, their faces, the brightness in them, gone from me or not, the brightest thing in the world. Bright as aurora.

I fall asleep, finally, I don't know how long, and as I fall I think I'm dreaming something, great dark rolling into great dark, slipping, weightless, I guess, but that's all. Then I think nothing, maybe engine hum, but nothing else. It's a fine state. A fine forever, as long as it goes.

Then something hits me, or takes me and smashes me into something, slams me down like a shot-glass in my sleep, snaps my head awake. I blink. Some kind of metal banging sound's going through me, the bones at the back of my spine feel it bang again, then I feel dropping. The plane does a belly-sick slide-and-drop and then it falls off the air and catches itself, and we jerk in our seats.

Everybody's awake now. The plane slips off the air again, drops again, smash-lurches, drops again. Bump and thump.

"What the fuck was that?" Henrick is looking at me.

The plane bangs again, drops again. Everybody grabs their arm-rests, holds on to their asses, looks at each other a long second, waiting, then it's banging again for real, harder, firecracker-finale banging, and the tube of the plane is twisting and buckling, insides buckling with it. It's hitting rocks maybe, smacking mountain maybe, but then we're still going somehow after that. It drops again, faster, faster, we tilt over on one wing, way over, we're strapped in hanging sideways in the air, turning, upside down, even faster, metal banging and wailing again like it's dying, thumping and tearing and none of us has a clue except that we died already, hit a mountain and died and kept going.

Tables drop and lockers pop open and bags and coats and phones and Playboys fly and more ripping and crumpling and laptops and boots and books and pieces of crap shoot by and somebody's keys smack me in the face and it all slams sideways and drops again, not long, but we start going faster than before, and a flight attendant flies by my face, skirt-up, something smacks me over the eye, I think the heel of one shoe, her other was off, I think, but I see her face as she flies away down the aisle, she looks at me, girl in a tornado.

Then we really hit something. Somewhere as you're dying there's more death, and whatever I thought we hit before, possibly, this we hit.

My brain shocks and my teeth buzz and everything gets punched and shaken at once between the balls and the belly and my spine, my shoulders drive up past my head, my throat drops into my ribs, my neck's up in my mouth broken inside out and the top of my head slams the bottom of my jaw, seats fly by, we fall and then fall further, hit something else, again, harder, louder than before, we slam and crack. I'm smashed in the face again, the lights out, a head flies by and the plane splits, cracks, a dark gap jagged line across the fuselage where it shouldn't be, arms and legs and blood and the head shoot by again, or another head, a bowling ball, this time I see his face.

I'm trying to think of his name as he flies away from me and I'm thrown back the other way, away, thinking, because thinking is slower than everything else now, that I should get to him and help him, and as I fly backwards I have to fight this, telling myself there's not much I can do to help a head.

The side of us hits something else, we seem to bounce. Lights come back on, explode, go off, glass pops, whatever the windows are made of. Everything goes darker than it was, cracking open, sliding, cold shooting in.

We're still slamming and sliding but I think I'm cold or bleeding, and I feel pressure, pulling on my belly and feet and the side of my head as we're still sliding and bouncing and slamming down something at horrible speed. I may be getting ripped apart but I see when I can look down, I think my head has not come off, or arms or legs.

A flood of snow is slamming in, everything changes to snow and cold ripping air, we're still going but we spin and crack open wider, still spinning. There's a body on me, or part of one, sweater in my mouth and drool or blood or worse, I can't push it off because we're spinning, then it flies off me anyway, then more bang-sliding, more snow shooting into my mouth, my nose, my eyes, through the lids no matter how tight I'm squeezing shut. We've filled with snow. Everything stops. So do I.

I'm buried. I can't breathe. Nothing. Not a molecule, or I can't work my lungs, suck all I want. Something feels broken, whatever is there, ribs. I feel snow packed in my mouth and nose. I snort and spit and cough my best but there is not much air still. It's snow mostly, but I'm partly breathing something but brain's not to be trusted, eyes either, nothing else either, I still feel like I'm still spinning, maybe still falling. I've stopped but I'm still flying through the air or it's wheeling past me, maybe. Maybe I'm falling. Maybe I'm headless or legless or gone.

I dig and push to get the hand jammed against my chest up under my chin and wriggle, shove my fingers up around my mouth to make a space so I'm not drowning, a little space around my mouth to breathe, an inch, two. I try to dig snow out of my mouth, blow it out of my nose. I'm still buried but I have these inches. I keep clawing but I can't move much of my arm.

I shove and push like crazy, then hunch and wriggle back, after more air, and I get more of my arm free and I dig out and pull my hand back and shove and suddenly I can twist and get my other arm out, it's in air. I start pulling and clambering, in the dark. I'm trying to see and there's nothing.

I push up and I hit a seat perched over me like a roof. I'm afraid I might be trapped under it and I shove with my legs as hard as I can until the seat and all the junk on top flips aside, and then air hits me, freezing cold, and I am breathing in buckets, sucking it in. It hurts at the top of every breath. Something's cracked in my chest or ribs or back or somewhere, all of it.

There's a patch of light below, through debris piled around me. It looks like more snow. I flop and fall towards it, then there's more light, or sort of light, pale, and more cold air. I tumble down a slope of something and hit some hard stuff but none of it badly and come to a stop again, sitting in the snow. I barely know what's down and what's sideways. I'm still spinning. Blood's washing through my ears, booming. I breathe, and hold on to the snow with my hands.

2

I CAN'T SEE where I am, but I know I'm outside the plane. Everything's outside the plane. The plane is pieces of shell, scattered. I slowly understand cold, snow, dark, moon, pieces of plane, seats, bags, bodies, new snow falling, line of trees, far away, maybe mountains past those, maybe, maybe we hit them and bounced this far. Everything's buzzing, spinning in my ears, loud buzzing silence. I think I stand up a second, hard to tell, but I fall back down, the ground smacks up at me, buzzing. The wind isn't blowing, which spooks me, because it's always blowing, in my head, anyway. If it isn't blowing now, I'm dead, and this is aftermath. Some get afterlife, some get aftermath.

I hold on, sitting another minute to stop drunk-spinning, look at the pieces stretching back, a black dotted trail of metal and I guess oil or somehow burn marks on the snow, if that's possible. More clumps of bags or bodies or pieces of bodies or seats or people's clothes, spread across the clearing, which I'm seeing is enormous, white. There's a ring of trees around us like the shore of a sea and we're an island of dead in the middle. I shake my head, work my jaw, thinking the buzzing changing to whining changing to ringing might pop out of my ears or stop if I do, but it doesn't. My jaw just clunks like a car door off its hinge. Behind the trail of stuff far back I can see trees are flattened and ripped where we came through.

I look the other way. I see a guy ahead now, far off. He stands up, flops over. Past him I see somebody else moving. He's crawling. He stops, falls flat against the snow. Then he tries to get up again. I see more pieces of broken shell spread over what looks like a mile. It can't be a mile.

Blood's still going through my ears, over the buzzing, in what sounds like a more and more determined way. My chest hurts more the more I breathe, but I still want to get more air in. I consider standing up again. I try to get up and I wobble but I take a step, ass-high in snow, I have to pull my leg up high, but I move. I think I'd know if anything was broken, and I don't think anything is, and I think if I'm breathing without screaming I didn't break ribs. I just got a talking-to.

I stumble and slide the rest of the way down the drift I'm in, land face-first. I get up again, and I'm on my feet, I'm up and staying up, and suddenly feeling the cold. I head for the guy who can't stay up. The crawling guy moves again, lying on the snow. He's feeling around looking lost, dizzy, like me. But he's further away.

I start toward them. I walk and walk, and before long I see they're further away than they looked. I keep on, pass more seats, more dead, each in their own craters, pocked into the snow. Some are half-sitting, some freezing, stiffening already. Others are flattened on harder snow, smashed-looking, worse on ice. Some are just pieces. I pass more bags, clothes, toothbrushes, razors, loose shoes, more pieces of metal, more dead, as far as I can see. The better my eyes work the further out I see them.

As I go the wind picks up. It's not a blast but it's more than it was, and there'll be more behind it. It starts picking up snow, getting louder. I stop a couple of times and check bodies I can get to. Nobody I check is alive. The guys ahead of me are the only things moving, and I keep making for them. I can't check them all.

I get near the first guy, finally. He's up again and trying to walk, in his boxers and socks, half-bloody from something. He looks broken, but it might be the way he's standing. He's hopping, bobbing, one arm and one leg sticking out crooked, trying to hoist his boxers up better, then he slips and flops back. He lands on his hand, screams in pain, or he's pissed off, or both. When I get up closer to him he's crying.

"I lost my fucking pants," he says. It's Ojeira. He's a tool-pusher. I look around, no blankets, nothing. Some bent seats a way off. I pull my sweater off, lay it on him.

"Can you move?" I ask him. He looks at his leg. I see it's purple, not just bloody, and twisted.

"Not this fucking leg. Not much. I think I could hop or something, in a minute. I'm going to sit a minute," he says. "It hurts like a fucker. Fucking shit."

He's mad at the plane for crashing, or the fucked condition of his bones. It has to hurt him, what I see.

"Fucking fuck." He's groaning and wincing and getting too pissed off. He's barely remembering to breathe, and I think with no clothes on he's going to freeze in a minute. The wind's rearing up on us, more. He is freezing. So am I.

"It's good it hurts," I say. "That's good." I look at him to see if he understands.

"Oh yeah? Good," he says. "I'm fucking terrific, then." I look around his shirt, what's there of it.

"What's bleeding?" I ask.

He looks down, lifts his shirt, his side and stomach are scratched and cut, some a little deep, but it doesn't look bad, it's just cuts. It's too cold to worry about infection. If there's a fucking bacteria alive in this it deserves whatever it can get. There's some bulge sticking out under his skin, some kind of hernia, guts or something. He doesn't notice it, and I don't say anything. I don't think it'll kill him. I don't know.

"Anything else?" I ask him. "Anything else bleeding?"

He shakes his head. "I don't fucking know yet. Fuck." He looks at me. "Ottway, yeah? What— John?"

I nod. "You're Ojeira, right?"

He nods. "Yeah. Fuck."

We look at each other. '*Why am I alive, and yet so fucked?*' he looks like he's thinking. He tries getting up again.

"Stay there for now, okay?" I say.

Ojeira nods again. He looks at his hand. Two fingers bent sideways, the whole hand blowing up, I see now. It looks dark purple, like his leg, or I'm guessing.

"Fuck me," he says. He tries to clench a fist, and almost gags.

"That hurts more than the rest of it," he says. He looks down at himself, his legs at different angles from the way he flopped down. He starts trying to set them right, and gives up, stops. He huffs in air, his eyes fill up. I think he's going to start crying again, but he just sits there.

"I'm going to sit. Another minute," he says.

"I'll come back. Stay here, okay?" I say. He doesn't have much choice. I look across the snow to the other guy. He's still crawling, trying to get on top of the snow, I see now he's been moving, he's just stuck in a drift so deep he's barely made three yards. I go over to him past bloody clothes and more bodies and parts of bodies. It's Luttinger, another tool-pusher. They're all tool-pushers.

"What the fuck," he says. "Fuck."

He finally gets up on harder snow and stays up, this time. Nothing seems wrong with him except he's unsteady. But no bones sticking out or limbs going the wrong way.

"Something rolled, broke open, I don't know. Slid a fucking mile." He touches his face, up by his eye and his forehead.

"I have any face left?" I can't tell much but it looks like he's just torn up. He still has a face.

"I think so. Yeah," I say. He's touching it.

"Feels like I scraped it all the hell off," he says. His clothes are half-ripped away, or burned away, from sliding across snow, or something, but he's got more on him than Ojeira. He looks at me.

"You okay?" he asks.

"Yeah."

He looks across to Ojeira.

"That guy's fucked," he says. Ojeira's gotten up, again. He's trying to walk. He looks pretty bad doing it. "Who is it?"

"Ojeira." Luttinger nods.

"Yeah. Shit." Luttinger says. "I'm Luttinger."

"I know." He looks at me, doesn't know me.

"I'm Ottway."

He looks at me again. He nods, not so glad to see me, suddenly.

"We should get him inside a piece of plane or something. Try to get him warm," I say. We both look around. There are more clumps in the snow, bodies or seats or wreckage, chunks of shell. Luttinger nods.

"Anybody else moving over here?" I ask him.

He shakes his head. "Nobody."

Of the ones we can see it's plain enough they're dead. I should start assuming everybody's dead.

We start back for Ojeira. It's harder going. I'm finding things hurting I didn't know were hurting before. The cold is numbing everything but sharpening everything at the same time. I stop at the first body we pass.

The guy has boots on. I pull them off, his jacket too, sweater. The guy's got insulated pants. I get those off him too. He looks familiar, but I don't think I know him. Luttinger doesn't say anything. I give the jacket to him. He looks surprised, but he takes it.

The other bodies we pass on the way to Ojeira are in t-shirts, or half-naked. I'm not understanding how clothes ripped off in the crash, but they did.

Luttinger and I reach Ojeira finally. He's glad to see us and pissed at the same time.

"I thought you weren't coming back," he says.

"We did, though," I say.

We get the pants and the boots on him, which seems to hurt him, but he manages. Luttinger looks at him shivering, and gives him the jacket I gave him before I ask him too. I get my sweater back on.

We get on either side of him and help him walk toward the nearest piece of shell we can get to. It's sticking up out the snow like a smokestack. I look for whatever piece I must have come out of and I can make out my tracks, where I think I came from, but whatever I fell out of looks tiny now, a little hunk of metal, couple of seats. I thought it was a more respectable piece of plane.

We haul for the smokestack but don't get much closer to it. We pass more bodies, then more again. We set Ojeira down to check them. They're gone, which we knew. But I see blankets, get one tied around me, give the other to Luttinger, then a little further I see bags ripped open, clothes spilled out, more sweaters and jackets. We get those on too.

We move again, haul a long time. We come up on something else. Some blood, dark in the snow, something else I can't identify, a piece of uniform wrapped in among it. It's half a pilot, or co-pilot, or navigator, one of those guys. I can't see anything that looks like a cockpit. He must have fallen out, or been thrown.

We keep going. We get to the smokestack, three times the distance it looked away. We set Ojeira down, huffing, look at the piece of shell. I see now there's no way into it unless we want to tunnel into it. Looking at it leaning, I think it's going to blow down anyway, if the wind gets any bigger, and kill us that way. I look back along the trail of wreckage and bodies and pieces of crap. I make out a bigger piece of plane, as far away again as this one was, which makes my heart sink. Nothing else looks much use to us.

The cold is drawing the life out of me. I think Ojeira will die if we don't keep trying get him into some kind of inside. We'll die too. I look at them.

"We should try to get to that piece." Ojeira looks at the distance, looks like he'd rather die here.

"Are you fucking kidding me?" Ojeira says. I just look at them. Luttinger nods. He starts hoisting Ojeira.

"Come on," Luttinger says.

We get Ojeira up again and start dogging through the snow for the next piece. It's an hour. I don't know, half an hour that feels like a day. We slog and pass dead and don't bother checking anymore. It's a long slog, with Ojeira hobbling and bumping us, but he's trying so hard to walk we don't say anything. We don't talk much at all, we're out of breath. We're head-smacked anyway. All we know to do is slog on in our lesser-mammal way.

We get up close. It's another piece of tube, but this one's flat in the snow, more or less. Beyond that there's another bump, looks like smashed cockpit, black holes for windshields, half-buried.

We make for the closer piece. There's no opening we can see, so we come around the blind side. There's a big hole, and more junk, more pieces and parts. More bodies, all around.

I see Tlingit, sitting in the snow, Reznikoff, an engineer, with him. They look wide-eyed, like they'd seen things they wished they hadn't, and then been beaten half to death. We must look the same. Tlinglit looks up, sees me. I'm happy to see him.

"You okay?" Tlingit asks. I nod. I can hear yelling from inside the tube. Tlingit nods to the hole in the fuselage. "More in there," he says. We step closer and see inside.

It's chaos, field-hospital. Everybody's groaning, gasping, swearing, yelling at once. Upside down seats on the ceiling, tilted. Wires, seatbelts, pieces of carpet, life-vests, torn cloth hanging down, broken seat bins, oxygen masks and tubes tangled under-foot, a boot with a leg sticking out of it, and blood, it looks like blood, everywhere.

Near the opening I see Feeny, I think his name is. He's miss-ing a hand, blanket around the stump. He's holding it up like if he had a hand he'd be giving you the finger. There's another guy next to him, leg gone, below the knee, somebody's tied it off for him but he's gasping, grunting, holding his thigh. Cismoski. Pretty sure. I never talk to anybody but I know names. Flora and fauna.

We get Ojeira propped against a piece of seat. I see Bengt further inside, staring up the aisle at Lewenden, who has his guts ripped open. He and Knox are holding little flashlights on him, yelling. Knox is a dry drunk, like the pastor, I think he is anyway. Lewenden's head is tilted to the side. It looks wrong on his neck somehow, as if the hole in his middle wasn't enough to worry about. I think about Tlingit saying all he needed was a neck-snapping.

As Knox's flashlight moves I see Henrick's there, kneeling over Lewenden, stuffing a blanket into his insides, but blood's still welling out. Henrick can't stop it, and Knox is yelling for somebody to do something, and they're yelling at each other and Bengt's yelling at both of them to stop Lewenden bleeding or he's dead. I go up, look at Lewenden. Lewenden sees me, doesn't look happy. He lays his head back, closes his eyes, groaning, somewhere low. He's out, I think.

Bengt suddenly realizes something, starts patting his pockets. He takes his light off Knox, looking around the junk thrown everywhere. He finally finds somebody's cell phone. He turns it on, starts trying to get a signal. Ojeira looks over at him.

"What the fuck is that for? Out *here*?" Bengt looks at Ojeira, keeps trying to dial. The thing is dead, too far from anything, too cold, smacked too hard, but Bengt keeps pressing buttons and looking at it like he's going to get an ambulance to come, and they might want directions. I'm still looking at Lewenden.

He's around again, but now he's shaking. He's going to die in a few minutes, I think. Nobody knows what to do. It's cold like you wouldn't believe. We're among dead and dying. Nobody's thinking well.

Henrick keeps trying to pad the hole. Trying to stuff the wound he moves something, something gives, somewhere, uncovers something and now there's blood flooding up like crazy, faster than before.

I don't know if it's artery or what but it's rolling up out of the cavity and as I step in closer Henrick moves the blanket again and it starts gushing. We try to block it, but it sprays over everybody. Everybody jumps back except Henrick and I, with our hands in Lewenden's insides. Henrick moves the blanket and it stops spraying, but it's still flowing out around and through.

Lewenden looks down. He's paler. He's draining, weaker.

"*Fuck*," Lewenden says. "*Fuck— Henrick.*"

"*Is there something we can use to tie off whatever the fuck this is?*" Henrick yells.

Lewenden fades out again, or just closes his eyes, groaning. But you can't see anything to tie off, it's just shooting out of some hole in something somewhere deep in there, so we stuff best we can but we know it's still leaking out from somewhere, just as fast. He's fucked in a way that's smarter than us.

Henrick looks at me, blinking blood out of his eyes, and Lewenden rolls around again, opens his eyes. He looks at Henrick and me, blood all over us.

"*Fucking do something, Henrick!*" Lewenden says, halfway to crying, and I don't blame him. I'd cry for him myself if I wasn't distracted. Henrick looks at Lewenden and doesn't come up with anything to say and Lewenden lays his head back and closes his eyes and it looks like he's passed out again, or he's just died. But blood's still coming and then I hear him groaning and grunting and mumbling something, praying, could be.

We hear him breathing, but it sounds hollow. He's going, I think. It's so much blood, and we can't imagine how we would put him back together, or hold him together, if he lived past the next minute anyway. A minute goes by like this, it seems longer.

We're just waiting, not knowing anything. Henrick lets go of the blankets, steps back, staring, with everybody else, we watch him, don't know what else to do.

Lewenden's suddenly awake again, gasping like he knows he's going and it woke him up. He starts trying to get up, as if he's going to be able to get up and walk away from it.

He looks at Henrick who just looks at him. He looks at me again, this time for help, he'll take it now. But I don't know what to do any more than Henrick does. I watch him fighting for air. He closes his eyes but not blacking out, it's like he's closing them in effort, and he keeps fighting for breath.

I put my hand on his chest and try to ease him from trying to get up which doesn't look like it's going to do him any good, and I look into his face in case he opens his eyes again, which he does. He's working for breath and gulping and looking terrified, and he's still thinking there's a way out of this, maybe, but there isn't. I try to stay in his eyes.

"You're going to die, okay? It's okay," I say.

Lewenden looks at me, in terror, then around at everybody else. They all stare.

"Look at me," I say, gentle as I can. "It's okay," I say again. I keep saying 'It's okay, it's okay,' looking in his eyes like I'm promising him something and I mean it, and I do mean it, it's the best I can do, and I stay with him best I can all the way, I take his hand, and he squeezes it close to breaking and I stay in his eyes with him, and he breathes and fights it until he dies. He stops moving, goes slack, his eyes go. I feel him leaving, I think. The blood tails away after a few seconds. Then it stops, too.

We all look at him. There's a silence. I look at the guys. They're all staring at him, spooked. Like hurt boys.

"Is this everybody alive?" I say. They all look at me like I shouldn't be talking yet, like I don't have the right. There should be a minute of silence, or some fucking thing.

"*Is this everybody?*" I say again. Nobody answers. We have Henrick, Bengt, Knox, Feeny, Cismoski, Luttinger, Ojeira, me.

"Eight inside, two more outside, yeah?" I say. It seems important to count.

I see Tlingit and Reznikoff have come in, standing in the opening. There might be others out in the snow somewhere, but it feels like we're the only ones left. I look around the plane.

"None of these others alive?" I ask.

Henrick finally answers. "I don't know."

There are maybe half a dozen dead-looking ones, a few more without question dead. I take Bengt's flashlight and go look at the ones who might be alive. They feel cold. I check pulses anyway, lift eyelids, though I know. I check anyway. I find one guy breathing, crumpled up halfway in what was an overhead, a piece of bulkhead's crunched down on him. He's still breathing when I get to him, but as soon as I see that he stops, just like that.

The others are still staring at Lewenden, or watching me, not doing anything. They don't know what to do.

"We should start a fire," I say.

They still look at me like I don't have a right to speak. Nobody moves, or answers. But Henrick and Tlingit nod.

"We should look for lighters or something. And anything that'll burn. Sooner the better."

Simple things. Dead or not dead. Artery or vein. Nobody moves yet. They stare at me. Hurt boys.

"*We have to get a fire going*," I yell, finally. "*So we don't die.*" They nod, more of them, but don't move.

"Any of you smoke? Any of you have lighters?" I ask. Bengt and Reznikoff feel their pockets, numb, but they don't have them now, if they did before. I start going through the pockets of dead guys, the crap everywhere, looking for a lighter.

Henrick's going through pockets of dead too, and the guys look at him like it's in bad taste. They expect it of me, but not him. He pulls out pens, other stuff. I find one lighter, a little plastic disposable. It lights.

"Okay. We need something to burn," I say. I talk like I'm talking to children. They're dazed. More than me. Luttinger and Henrick look at the seat cushions, same as I'm doing.

"Those'll burn," I say.

I nod toward the wreck trail behind us. "I saw a lot of broken wood back there, the crash scattered it," I say. "Let's start it with these if they'll go, then we'll ferry wood up. Okay?"

Henrick nods, Luttinger too. Bengt and Knox and Reznikoff all nod, finally, then the others. The ones who can move start tearing out loose cushions and piling them in the snow by the opening.

After a minute they look at Luttinger and me wearing jackets. Henrick goes and finds one, loose. The others have to pull them off dead guys, but they do it. Nobody touches Lewenden's jacket. Too bloody, or we just don't want to.

We get as many jackets as we can and pile them on Ojeira and the other injured like sleeping bags. I get whatever blankets I can, whatever other jackets, a couple, for slings to drag wood back with. Henrick pulls a bent piece of panel out of the way to make more room for Ojeira and the others and he finds a medical kit. He looks sorry to see it.

"We could have fucking used this before," he says. Not that an ace bandage and a gauze patch would have saved Lewenden. He knows that.

24

We've gotten some cushions out, enough. We drag them outside. I try lighting them, and they flare up like torches, six feet high. You'd think they'd be fire-proof. Good they aren't. Some of the guys cheer, whoop. It's something. We're alive. We have a fire. They seem to be waking up, a little. We stand as close as we can to it, taking what heat we can, but it isn't enough. I want to eat it, or climb into it, lie down in it, go to sleep.

"Some of us should stay here and keep this going. The rest of us should see what wood we can get out there."

I turn and head out. Henrick's right behind me. Luttinger and Tlingit and Knox and Bengt follow. Reznikoff stays behind with Ojeira and the others. Outside the reach of warmth, away from that minute of fire, it's even colder than before, darker in the shadows. But there's still moon on the snow. There are big ceiling clouds moving, and snow coming down heavier again. We keep walking, past more chunks of plane. More baggage and dead.

We look into any piece of wreckage big enough to have an inside, yell in, in case somebody's alive. Nobody. But we see more dead and parts of dead, in seats. We look at bigger pieces to see if one's a better shelter than where we are. One looks better than the others, leaned into the snow so it almost has a door, but it's too small a space inside to get everybody into. It's the one with the most dead, anyway, jammed up in piles, somehow.

We come up on the cockpit, finally. It looks like a crushed hard-boiled egg. I duck under a hole, shove my way in. The frame's bent and almost folded in on itself but I can squeeze through the opening. As I shove in Henrick's coming through the hole behind me. I wriggle and push the rest of the way in.

Not a lot of light. No sign of the pilots, no bodies. No pieces of uniform like I saw outside. Henrick gets through the door, we fumble around in the dark for anything that looks like survival stuff, or signal stuff, some kind of transponder thing, but neither of us has any idea what we're looking for.

For some reason we expect to find a flare gun or an emergency kit, tents or rations or something. No such things. We try to make sense of the piles of twisted wires and ripped metal, try to find whatever switches would have anything to do with the radio, but nothing's powering on anyway no matter how many switches we flip, everything's fucked. We look at each other.

"You see any sign of the pilots out there?" Henrick asks. I nod.

"Half of one." It strikes Henrick as funny.

"The other half's fucking hiding in shame," he says. I nod. We fall quiet.

"Better move," I say. We crawl back out.

Outside I see Luttinger and the others waiting for us. They've slogged ahead a little and they're jumping around. Too cold to stand still. Back at the piece of plane I see flames going up higher. It looks like they're throwing more seat cushions on. It roars up, must be fifteen feet of flame.

"We better hurry with the wood or that'll be gone in five minutes," I say.

Henrick nods. We huff up to catch the others. Luttinger falls in alongside us, when he get to him. The rest of the guys are already tromping ahead in the cold, strung out on the snow, staring into the dark to where the broken trees are.

I keep looking out to either side of us, at every dark clump we pass to see if any of them is moving. None of them is. Like before I can't go out to check every one of them or I'll die doing it. The others will too. So I hope they're dead, and I'm not leaving anybody alive we could have helped. You hope funny things.

We keep going until we see the broken trees trailing back from the crash. Massive chunks of wood, and big and little branches. We're still what looks like a few football fields or more from the trees but pieces of tree got thrown here somehow as we came through. I'm trying to imagine it and I can't, but here they are.

Everybody starts gathering wood up, dumping it in the blankets and jackets, loading up their arms. I lay a blanket out, load it up. Henrick and some of the others take their jackets off to bundle wood in, which is brave in this cold. It doesn't take long, we can't carry much. Henrick heads off, dragging what looks like a big load for him. He isn't the biggest of us, but off he goes. Tlingit and Luttinger and the others follow him, head for the orange pinprick of the fire in the distance.

I find myself staring at the snow, getting breath, as they go ahead of me. I almost see the shape of the pieces of the plane from here, like I could put it together. I look another part of a minute maybe, and I see them getting ahead of me.

I get going, dragging my load of wood. After a minute or two more I feel like I've been walking in snow for a year, added to the haul before, added to falling out of a plane, and now I've got a blanket full of wood that weighs more the further I drag it.

Far from the fire like this, even with the wind getting up, it's surprisingly peaceful. Snow is coming in still heavier and more clouds are coming over too I think. We're on a giant white slab getting buried by the hour, all new snow. Sounds hopeful.

I pass a dead guy a little ways off, and another. I don't know if I passed them on the way out, my eyes are adjusting. I look further out to the sides, I see a big flat shadow of cloud moving away across the snow letting more moon down, and I see more dark clumps, more dead, a field of dead, more than I'd seen before.

I stop walking again for a moment looking at the bodies. Without my footsteps in the snow or the others' it's incredibly silent, even with the wind. The buzzing's gone from my ears, I realize, the pounding too, or I think it is.

I think I hear snow moving behind me. I turn, look back. I don't see anything, just dark dead dots in the snow. But I keep looking back, another second, further into the dark. One of the dead is moving, it looks like, now, trying to get up or worse, shaking. He looks bad. I let go of the wood and start walking back to him. Then I start running.

"*Hey!*" I'm shouting, "*I'm coming— I'm coming!*"

I shout and run, as hard as I can, because he's shivering, convulsing, I think, some kind of spasm. He's dying his last, maybe, but he still looks like he's trying to get up. It's hard to see, just this clump shaking in the snow. The sight's frightening, I don't know why. But I want to get to him before he dies, if that's what he's doing. So I keep lunging and huffing through the snow, yelling, and he keeps shuddering, retching or something, fighting to stand, I can't tell.

"*Hey—*" I yell again.

Then he seems to split in two, or I see something jumps off him, half a second. It looks up at me, then jumps back on him. Some fucking thing, an animal. "*Hey!*" I yell as loud as I can, as if this guy, who I realize is dead, probably, cares. But I yell, and run faster.

"*Get the fuck off him!*" I yell.

Its head comes up, looks at me. It's a wolf, ripping at the guy or his jacket, and I see now I'm closer the guy is dead if he was alive at all. It was the wolf I saw moving. The wolf just stares at me.

I charge at it, screaming. I don't know why I'm charging, but the wolf stares at me, watches me come at him. I'm thinking he

28

killed the guy, he was alive and this fucker killed him, or he was dead and he's got food on him, or he's at his guts, I don't know, but I'm charging, yelling, and expecting him to twitch or flinch and turn tail and jump off but he isn't moving, he's just watching me.

Then I'm hit sideways. I think I've been hit by a piece of plane, I'm in a blur, slammed in the snow with my eyes open, snow jammed up my nose, under my lids again and something's digging and dragging into my back and dragging me, and somewhere in getting tossed upside down I think it's the wolf, but it can't be, and I understand it's another wolf, locked onto the back of my jacket, or my back, I can't tell, but it's tunneling into me best it can, and I'm face down in the snow. I shove myself up, get half up off the snow almost standing, but he hangs on. I pick him up with me, or most of him, hanging by his teeth. I hear him growling.

Then I'm hit again, at the back again but the other side, up under my arm, the other one's hanging off me now, I'm standing with two of them hanging on to me by their jaws, and they aren't letting go, and I'm trying to swat with my elbows and grunt and I can't see them but I think one drops behind me where I can't see him or get at him but as I twist I smell fur and his breath and I finally get around enough to see the top of his head and his ears, and I smell more fur, more hot breath, he's buried in my armpit burrowing his teeth in. The other is still off me. He's bouncing left and right behind me looking for the next place to latch on while I spin the one still on me around, swinging, frantic, trying to shake him.

I can't tell if the one still on me has really got his teeth in me or he's mostly eating jacket. I feel his teeth, I think, but I don't know how far they're in me, or if they're in me or just hurting. I'm still swinging and trying to stop him getting leverage to really bite. I'm trying to smash him harder now that I can see something and I try to twist further and I pull his ear and I bash and bash with my elbow at his head, as hard as I can, like I'm trying to crack his skull. I'm waiting to hear a cracking sound, as if I'm going to be able to hit as hard as that.

I hear jacket ripping and I feel muscle or something tearing under my arm and he seems to come loose, but he bounces up again, gets a new bite on my back. I'm still praying he's getting more jacket than me. He's snorting, growling, but he is not flinching except to get a better grip and get the damn jacket out of his way or get more muscle. It's hurting enough, stabbing sharp. I think he must be in me by now.

I look up as the other one hits me again, on my leg. I kick as hard as I can before he can sink in too deep. He gashes me, feels like, but he comes loose. He took a piece or didn't, I don't care, if he's off me. It hurts, but in the cold it all does, he's got my whole leg for all I know and I'm nothing but spinal cord on my back, I'm a meatless stack of bones fighting when I'm already gone into something's mouth, nothing to save, but still fighting as if there is.

The one I kicked off jumps up at me again. I get my arm up in time, barely, and he locks on my arm in front of me, I get a face-full of his teeth. His breath's hot. I spin again, the other still on my back, and I get my other arm up and smash him as hard as I can, again.

He lets loose and tries to get another hold but he misses the bite and drops, and somehow the one who came at my face drops. I think I finally pulled his ear half-off, something came loose, maybe fur. He drops and I spin. I've got the two of them in front of me, and I can see them both for the first time.

I don't think of running because I know they'd run me down and in the half-second I think that, I'm thinking, '*Okay, we'll calm down now, we'll look at each other and we'll settle,'* and as I think that they come at me again. I realize I can die now or do otherwise.

I charge at the one in front and roar and try to seem big like they tell you to do with animals and he leaps up and goes for my side, but he misses.

I step after him and kick the side of his head as hard as I can. He backs off a step. I charge again because I can't run and I can't stand there. He almost gets my whole leg in his jaw this time but I snap back. He grazes off. I get my leg out, he doesn't get a hold. I kick at his face again, harder, and he hesitates this time. He doesn't come in at me. But the other one jumps up over my arm and closes his mouth on my face, half over my eyes.

I get my hands up trying to wedge him away but I fall back in the snow with him on me, locked on my face and squeezing. The other one's on my chest suddenly, trying to get up under my neck. I think my arm's in his way. He jumps off, I can't see anything with this one's mouth over me and I'm wondering as I try to leverage him off when his teeth will puncture bone and my skull will crack in two, and I feel the other one land on me again.

I'm dead now, I think, I'm pushing and kicking but it feels like digging in water, they're going to get into me and go through me now and that will be that. I'm pushing their weight and trying to twist away but one's on my leg and I can't. A few more seconds, maybe.

I hear yelling, stomping, coming across the snow, guys charging and boots thumping, heavy thuds coming through the wolf on me to my chest. My knuckles and head are getting smashed with heavy branches, lumps of wood. I'm getting bone-break beaten as well as getting raked by wolves.

I see Henrick with a piece of wood, swinging, Luttinger and Tlingit too, the others, all smacking hell out the wolves and me with them, but I still have the wolves on me. Then Tlingit rears back and swings his log like a bat and knocks one right off me. Henrick swings his down on the other from over his head. It bounces down and jumps loose. The wolves hop away and turn and face us.

I try to get to my feet. All I do is slip over backwards and hit the snow. I pull up to see where the wolves are. They stare at me and at Henrick and Luttinger and Tlingit and the others, standing here with their logs, ready to swing. They stare at us and breathe, a few breaths, half a dozen, maybe.

Then they just turn and trot off, into the dark. I fall back on the snow. I feel less than safe lying there instead of up watching the wolves go. But I can't hold myself up anymore.

My knuckles and arms are throbbing where the guys and the wolves hit me. My face and back are throbbing and numb, or bleeding, so are my legs. My face feels like it's had nails driven into it, as if teeth are still in my skull. I want to get a hand up to see what's left of me but I can't, at the moment, lift my hands. I stay flat on my back, looking up, breath misting up, away, while Henrick and the others either stare at me or stare into the dark where the wolves went. Luttinger looks at me, waiting to see if I want to get up, or if I'm going to.

Finally I move, get up on my feet. Henrick and the others look at me like I'm not supposed to get up, because I should be dead. It's so cold I can't tell if I'm in pieces or not. I think they didn't get that much of me. Things are hurting everywhere, but I don't seem to be gushing blood, and I don't feel like falling over again, or at least it doesn't seem a necessity. That makes me think I'm not bucketing blood into my shoes without knowing.

I look down anyway. My pants are half-dark with blood. I feel them sticking to the new blood and the blood that's freezing already. But I still feel like they didn't get anything decisive of me. I feel okay.

Henrick drops his piece of wood and starts prodding and patting me, trying to lift my jacket to see how bad it is. I'm looking too, but I'm looking over his shoulder and past the rest of the guys out toward the dark, wherever it is they went. The wolves are still gone, as far as I can tell. Or just gone from where I can see them.

There's enough moon that I see their tracks all over where they were jumping on and off me. My blood's in the snow, and their tracks past that leading away, toward the trees, I think. But the tracks disappear too soon to say, and there's nothing else, I'm not hearing anything. I look left and right across the trees. I find myself staring at one particular point, then another. Why those points and not others I don't know, but. I still don't see them. They might be there and I just can't pick them out against the trees.

Who knows. I want to tell myself I have a clue or a guess because the tracks seemed, maybe, to lead that way, but I don't have any such thing. I look at the snow where I was down, and the blood, again, and I nod to Henrick and Tlingit and the others, which I mean as thanks, and they nod, which means okay.

"Let's get back," I say.

I start back across for the load of wood I dropped. I can feel them looking at me like I'm crazy, but we need the wood, and I'm alright. Henrick and Tlingit come with me and help.

We get it all up, and the others have theirs picked up again. They're waiting for us to catch up. Henrick walks next to me, Tlingit on the other side. They're both watching the dark like I am.

"You're okay to walk back?" Henrick asks.

"Yeah. I'm okay," I say. And we join the others and get walking, and keep walking, lugging our loads. It seems further than before back to the shell, and the fire that was up so huge looks to be down to a little glow by now, and far away. We keep looking around us, right and left and back as we go, and we go quicker than we did before.

3

I'VE KNOWN WOLVES, when I was younger. I met them on hunts, going out with my father. Or going after my father, un-invited, tracking him. He was afraid of wolves, and hated them for it, and made it his business to punish every one he met for it. He knew he would drive them so bad one of them would kill him one day, I suppose, and he would make them all pay in advance. Or they were something else to him, I don't know what, darkness or death or fear, all the worst things he was, he saw in them. Which none of them deserved as far as I could see, any more than any of us did. He took money to kill them some of the time like his father did and made it his mission the rest of the time.

He got into blood feuds, contests, long wars, because it wasn't always as simple a thing as him having a rifle and them not. There were wolves that would fox him and wolf him and fool him, curse him like he cursed them. His bullets would miss them, or go through them, they'd get out of traps, jump out of deadfalls, all of which they did to vex him, keep him poor, drive him mad. People call them ghost walkers, after all.

"The wolf's the only animal who'll avenge his brother," he'd say. And leave me to wonder what he meant.

But I've watched them, tracked them to watch them, met them eye to eye in the woods. A wolf will never do what these just did to me, as good as never, unless he's rabid, which these weren't I think, or unless you give it nothing else it can do. You have to be determined to make a wolf do that, you'd have to be trying, like my father did. Even then he'd rather snarl at you and lope away or make friends or stare you to death. Unless you're another wolf. Then he'll kill you as soon as look at you if you aren't one of his, and you're in his place of business.

So I did something to get hit like I did, I think. I lost my mind, probably, the wolf was after some jerky or a candy bar and I had to charge at him and get my back skinned off. I've never seen a wolf at a dead man, but I've heard stories. Every hunter has stories. Maybe they smelled wolf on me, from years ago, and didn't like it. Maybe they thought I was a wolf, and not one of theirs. We don't belong here after all. Maybe they smelled my father.

We finally come up to the heat of the fire, what's left of it. Reznikoff and Ojeira and the others we left behind have passed out and it's low, sputtering in the wind. We get it loaded up with the wood and I stoke and stoke it then we all get it stacked up until it's roaring again, which is stupid, I know, but a fool-headed fire it is.

I try to soak what heat is coming off the fire into my body. I thaw a little and I start to feel where I'm bitten and gashed, and I'm dizzy again. Everything drifts and shifts as heat comes up at me. I'm expecting to fall face-first into the fire. But I don't, I just weave and stare at the flames and try to think about where we are. We all huddle into it.

"That feels fucking good," Bengt says, huffing and blowing.

"It fucking does," says Henrick.

36

"That's the touch of a good woman, right there," Tlingit says, and they all huff and groan, laugh a little, even Knox, who's wide-eyed.

"Don't talk about that shit out here," Henrick says. Then he falls quiet, thinking about what he doesn't want to think about. The others do the same.

"We're not dead yet, boys," I say. They all shrug, laugh again, still thinking.

"Not yet," Henrick says. It's either hopeless or tough, depending on how you hear it. I remember sitting on the snow with a rifle in my mouth and I remember fighting the wolves off, or trying to, and when I thought they had me it felt like a cliff I didn't want to go off. I didn't want them to take what I didn't want to give them, I suppose. I remember the others looking at me after Lewenden like hurt boys, babies, and I look at them standing at the fire now. Maybe I don't want to leave them alone here. Maybe both.

I thaw more and it hurts more. I leave the fire and I go toward the piece of plane. The others come in too for now. Fire or not we all want to be inside something. Nobody wants to be out alone.

Inside the piece of shell there's glow from the fire coming in. It almost feels like we've made camp, just by setting fire to something. Ojeira and Cismoski are still alive, buried under jackets. They wake up when we come in. I think about carrying them out to the fire but they don't look too bad. Staying in shelter with the fire taking edge off the air kept them above freezing I guess, or close enough.

I find one of the flashlights they were using for Lewenden and wedge it into an arm-rest. I start to take my jacket off, or try to, to see what the bites are like. Henrick and Tlingit help me with the jacket. It's sticking to my shirt, blood dried and frozen, and the shirt's sticking to me. Luttinger and the others are watching. They still stare like I should be dead. Henrick holds up my jacket to show me. It's in shreds, bloody. The shirt is the same. I see why they're staring. I don't suppose I look well.

As the air is hitting my back I'm wondering how deep it goes there, and as I move more I start to feel how bad they bit me and where. It feels worse on my right side, on my back, but it still doesn't feel fatal. Henrick pokes at it and wipes blood off with snow which doesn't feel too marvelous but somehow isn't too bad, nothing like as bad as I was afraid. I put a hatchet through my knee once, chopping wood, and my mother half-fainted, my knee-bone hanging out, big flap of skin, blood filling my shoes. But it barely hurt at all, it felt like a little cut. One of those things.

There's a piece of window still in its hole near where I'm standing. I look at my face reflected by the light from the fire and the flashlight and I see more gashes and I remember the one that was clamped onto my face. So I am not pretty. Maybe I do look dead. Maybe I'm a ghost walker.

I remember too, now that my shirt is off and I see Henrick and Tlingit and Luttinger looking, the little pock-marks, the old holes in my chest. I look away before anybody says 'How'd you get those holes in you?' Henrick looks at me like that's what he's thinking. 'The chicken pox,' I'll say, if he asks me. But he gets on with the job, and the others don't say anything, either.

I get my pant leg up and that looks a good bit worse. But they didn't seem to get any tendons or arteries or anything. I walked the way back, after all, and maybe because of the cold, bleeding has stopped all over. Some other digs and nips, but my face is there, for better or worse, and I'm not dying tonight. Not from this. In a certain number of days I could die from the bites in my leg. That could get infected and kill me. I wonder if the cold really kills infection, or if I was making that up. Maybe I'll need my leg whacked off, but I'm thinking by the time I'd die that way five other things will have killed me. I've got four or five days I think of free ride, anyway. Better than some of us here. Better than the ones who've gone.

Henrick puts all kinds of peroxide and triple ointment and bandages on me from the kit we found after Lewenden died, and he starts winding me up like a mummy. I admit it feels better, as he winds it on.

Everybody's quiet, watching Henrick package me up. Then they're looking out at the dark and they're thinking about the wolves, I can see. As if freezing to death before we have a chance to starve to death before anybody finds us in the dark isn't occupation enough. Finally I see Bengt look at me.

"What the fuck happened? They just jumped on you?" Bengt asks. I don't know any more than he does.

"I must have pissed them off," I say.

"Yeah, you must have," he snorts. He's either laughing at me, or mad at me for making the wolves dislike me, so now we have to worry about how much. Knox just stares, still wide-eyed.

"They were spooked, probably. Defending themselves," I tell them. They all look at me as if they wouldn't be surprised, but none of them really believes it, because they're too scared. I'm already the camp murderer, the ghoul who goes to the funerals, the shadow of death, the camp curse, the one who sent off Lewenden, the witch of the ice and snow.

"I tried to run one off a dead guy. He probably had food on him. The other was just protecting that one. More than likely they won't bother us again."

I look at them to see if they're going to keep worrying about the wolves. We sit a minute, and sure enough we're all sitting there worrying, about wolves and being alone on the snow with no doors to lock, and Lewenden and the other dead, because they could be us, and the cold, and missing hands and chopped-off feet and the possibility we might die here, after one or two increasingly uncomfortable days that'll bind worse and worse until we die, and that this, looking back, might be the easiest minute we'll have. We might never see people we love again, we've deserted them, they'll be alone in the world, and what have we done to protect them, if we never come home?

I know they're thinking of that, because even when a plane hasn't dropped them in the snow, that's what most of them are thinking about when they stare across the bar, probably when they try to fall asleep. It's what I used to think about, still do, pointless as that is. That's the look they have now, but worse. If they die here, they've failed loved ones, fucked up mortally, and no remedy forever. We sit there, thinking, because what we're used to doing is either worrying or resenting, and if we ever thought about that we'd realize when we're doing that we're really thinking about what ties us to this earth, or doesn't. And now we're dangling and wondering.

I look for my watch suddenly, but it's gone.

"What time is it?" I say. Reznikoff looks at his.

"Nine o' clock," he says. "Little after." Like it matters. We sit another moment.

"It feels later, doesn't it?" I say.

Tlingit laughs his funeral laugh.

"It fucking does," he says. "I thought it was quarter-past fucked."

Then all of us are laughing our marooned dead asses off. Two hundred dead guys not counting us, we're hanging on like ghosts laughing in the wind. I remember some poem my wife would say, something about somebody dying into the hands of the wind. Like we are.

We fall quiet again. I see Henrick looking at Lewenden, and the other dead sitting around us. We're sitting with corpses, and barely thinking of it, till now. I see the others looking too.

Reznikoff looks at Ojeira and the other two, Cismoski and Feeny, passed out or sleeping, again. He goes and puts his hand on Cismoski suddenly, touches his face. Then he looks up.

"He's dead." We all look over at him, shine the light. Cismoski's blue-white.

"I thought he was going to be okay." Bengt says. Ojeira wakes up, looks around, so does Feeny. They see us staring, realize Cismoski's dead, next to them.

"So did I," Knox says, staring.

Everybody's staring at Cismoski. We should be expecting this kind of thing to happen but we aren't. We haven't understood where we are.

"We should move him outside, maybe. Lewenden too, and the rest," I say. They look at me. Feeny looks uncomfortable, next to a corpse. Ojeira does too.

"Yeah?" I say.

"Then we look for food, okay?"

Nobody wants to pick up the dead and carry them, but nobody wants to spend the night with them. We move them, lift them out one by one as gently as we can past the fire out to the snow. There's nothing stranger than carrying dead, how their weight feels, how they move in your hands and how you feel they're alive. I held a bird when I was a kid that felt like that, fell out of the sky, like us. I held it and thought of my mother, somehow, a little bird.

Henrick and I take Lewenden out, and as I tilt to get down the slope through the opening Lewenden's head rolls just like he's decided to turn his head and look up at me. I look at him like I'm sorry, when I'm over the shock, and I am.

I don't know if he was married, or had kids, I didn't think so, and I should have said something when he was going if I had thought of it, like 'We'll make sure so-and-so is okay,' or 'We'll tell so-and-so you love them,' but as he was going I didn't think of it, I only do now, carrying him. We get him laid down and get all of them all out, lay them in the snow as decently as we can, and it makes us feel better.

We come back and everyone stands, more silent than before, back by the fire to feed it and get warmer again.

"Anybody see any food?" I ask.

"Must be something," Henrick says.

We pull ourselves away from the fire again and look for what food there is by what light there is. We find frozen dinners, pieces of sandwich, power-bars, juice-cans, water-bottles, frozen, bits and pieces. A couple of dozen bags of peanuts and pretzels. We count and divvy and try to figure how long we can make what we have last.

"Maybe we can hunt, somehow," I say. "Stretch this out." What we'll hunt, and what we'll hunt with, I have no idea. Water isn't a problem, we're walking on it. We take a little food to Ojeira and Feeny, make sure they aren't freezing. Then we get back to the fire, stoke it again, try to get warmer. We all eat a little, handfuls of peanuts.

"How many more days until it's all night up here?" I ask.

"Three more?" Henrick says. "Four, maybe? It's about an hour of day tomorrow, I guess. Less the next day."

"Company will probably come for our bodies in the spring," Tlingit says.

"If then," Ojeira says.

Everybody nods. We've been busy with not freezing or dying and we haven't even thought out loud about it.

"The company isn't going to send out fifty planes to search half a million square miles in the dark, neither is anybody else. They just aren't, except the insurance company, if they have insurance, and that'll be for the plane, not for us. We'll get a piper-cub and a guy with binoculars, maybe some samaritans, good bush neighbors. They'll try a few days," I say.

"I know with the amount of daylight and the amount of empty space if we were off-course at all when we came down, all they're going to find if they ever finally find us is wreckage and frozen bones, and empty peanut-bags, good as likely." I look at the guys.

"So we gather our shit, as much food as we can find, and walk out," I say. Most of them nod, after a while. They're afraid to stay and afraid to go.

"The plane is shelter though," Knox says.

"It is. But we'll die in it before anybody comes." I look at them.

"Okay? We get up first light, use whatever daylight we get, walk west," I say.

Nobody says we might just as well walk north, and I don't know which way we're more likely to hit ocean and help. I'm only guessing west. I don't know what mountains I thought I saw or which side of them we're on. And what's west is going to be a guess too because the sun isn't going to get much over the horizon anyway before it drops. I'm hoping it'll come up and drop true south, I'll see it, and I'll guess. They aren't arguing.

"Okay," Henrick says. The wounds on my face and back are hurting me more, my leg too. I still take it as good sign. Throbbing a little.

We split into watches to keep the fire going. Some of the guys try to pull on more jackets and extra thermals from people's bags, or from bodies, and try to sleep. I'm supposed to be one of the injured, as we're calling them now, but I go out and sit up with Bengt and Knox and tend the fire anyway. The rest go inside the piece of plane, after clinging to the fire a while. They still feel better inside.

I look at the white around us, and the trees, and before long I stop looking at the snow and the clearing and I just stare out. I watch the dark, and watch where I think the trees would be. Bengt falls asleep, but neither he nor Knox sleep for long. I watch them wake up in shifts, lie there, scared of dying or cold or starving or the wolves, and try to go back to sleep. Knox sleeps as near the fire as he can without setting light to himself, still looking worried. Bengt gives up, finally, sits up.

"You should sleep," he says to me. "I can tend the fire."

I don't want to sleep. We tend the fire and I watch. I don't want to watch, because I don't want to think about whatever it is I'm watching for. Things I don't want to make happen by watching for them. Making the air think of them. But I watch shadows of pieces of junk and wreck all around, bodies, snow between us and the rest of the world. I stare and stare.

Before long I see them, small dark lines. They're flitting between the edge of what I see and what I can't, dark in dark. I stand up to see better. Bengt looks out, trying to see what I'm looking at, not that my eyes are any better, but I'm looking harder. Bengt sees them too now. He kicks Knox, who looks at us, freezing. He gets up.

Inside, the guys who are trying to sleep but aren't see us standing. They come out too, except for Feeny and Ojeira. We're all standing, stone-still like a pack, watching the same moving dark lines on the snow we don't know how far away because you can't tell how far away anything is.

But they circle closer. I see them, the two from before maybe, with more, now, eight or ten together, dark lines, circling, looking at us, it looks like. Drawn by the fire, I'm wanting to think, or curiosity, they smell us and wonder what we are. They realize the fucker they ran into before hasn't left yet. Pay him a visit, see him off. We're a splinter, maybe, something you want out.

They draw in closer, then closer again, cutting around to us, watching, and we see them better and better, as well as you can see smoke at night in the distance, so barely at all. We watch. Nobody says anything.

They circle in closer again, turn toward us this time. My hackles go up, my guts get tight. One of them cuts out of the group. I see him against the snow, black fur, it looks like, and bigger than the others.

He sits staring at us, twenty yards out. A little glow from the fire reaches him. The others stop circling, sit down too. They all stare at us, seconds slow-slapping by, my pulse going in my head, my neck.

I'm trying to see if I can tell which ones were on me, and I can't. Or I'm not sure. There are two smaller ones who look like they were the ones. I don't know. I'm not naming them. I don't mean to but I find myself staring at the big one, in front. I have the feeling he's staring at me.

Then he gets up and trots off, suddenly. And just as suddenly the others get up and trot off after him, toward the trees where they came from, disappear. The guys look at each other, at me.

"What the fuck were they doing?" Henrick asks. I look out, still watching, to see if they're circling back in.

"They're curious," I shrug. "We're on their turf." This seems to make sense to everybody, but somehow it makes things seems worse. They nod, turn back to the shelter of the hull. Bengt looks at me.

"If we're on their turf, are they going to make us get off?"

"They might be passing through," I say. "Most likely they'll leave us alone."

"You said that before," Bengt says. And they have left us alone, I want to say. But I don't want to argue.

"We're walking out tomorrow. That's all we need to think about. Okay?"

Everyone looks back, thinking about going back inside. But as safe as that seemed before, now nobody wants to leave the fire, as if the fire gives us anything. But Henrick and the others go back in, looking back at us. I can see through the little windows everybody trying to settle back into their places. We stay awake, out here. Nobody sleeps for a long time.

4

THERE'S WHISTLING, RATTLING, creaking, clanking. I blink awake. The sun is up its little bit, grey. Snowing heavier, now, and sideways. The wind is up too, blowing through the wreckage, sheets of broken metal and sheets of plastic panel flap back and forth, pieces of debris drift by, some pamphlet about something, somebody's scarf blows across the snow. With everything blowing and ticking and knocking it seems quieter than it did before, somehow. The fire's out, I'm unhappy to see, and Knox and Bengt are sleeping on the snow near me.

I look to see if they're frozen to death or just sleeping. They're sleeping, I think, or in comas, but if I woke up they will too, probably. But that's miracle enough, because letting the fire go out was stupid enough to kill us. Maybe it didn't go out that long ago.

I'm unhappy it's daylight, and we've wasted it already, and that it's colder again with the wind. I want to start the fire again but I hope we won't be here that long. My eyes are sticky and burning from frost or wind and whatever scraping they got from the wolves. When I slept at all I would see them over and over in blurs and wake up again.

I look out as far as I can see across the snow in the grey light. No wolves, which is what I was looking for, and I feel like a fool because I know I'm afraid instead of thinking.

Everybody but Ojeira's still asleep I think. Ojeira's in the opening, looking at the wind, anxious. I can't see anybody else in the plane. I get up and twist around, trying to put my spine and my ribs back where they belong. I jump up and down to get warmer. I shake Bengt and Knox, because sleeping in the cold too much longer they'll die. They have to move.

They look at me, blinking, with we're-still-alive looks, and the cold hits them and they hunch over and rock and yell out, get themselves up, saying 'shit' and 'fuck' as many times as somebody can in a few seconds. I look at the snow, all around, again. I walk out a ways, daring myself, doing what I don't know. But I think if I walk out further and up a rise and look out and see no wolves I'll know what a fool I am.

I don't go all that far before I stop. I see tracks, as my eyes get used to the white. Big tracks, big paws, all around us. Filling over with snow. This isn't where they were when they were staring at us, these are closer, they were sniffing us out, I think. I look back to the plane, measuring the distance, and the snow to left and right. Then I see brown dots and blotches here and there, all over, not covered by snow yet. They pissed out territory all around us, and I wonder what else they're going to do.

I take a few steps up the rise, out where we laid the dead, not too far off. I see red smeared across. It doesn't look like it's from any of the dead we brought out, we didn't drag them. I look back at the plane again, around at the snow, nothing moving, just Knox still jumping, Bengt taking a piss. Ojeira's still by the opening, watching me, still anxious.

I go out to the red snow, trying to figure out what I'm seeing, then I see Luttinger. I come up on him. He's all ripped, inside out, black and red, blood, frozen blue-white, the rest of him. Snow is piling up at his edges as the wind blows at him. It's started to cover him.

He came out to take a leak in the night and this is what happened to him. I think what an idiot, to come this far out, then I see the gully in the snow, red in it fading away, where they dragged him from. I don't know why. Like an angry thing, dragging, maybe.

I lean closer to Luttinger to be sure he's all the way gone, I suppose. He is. I feel stupid checking. Henrick's stepped out from the piece of plane past Ojeira. He sees me standing over Luttinger. He starts out to me through the wind. When he gets here he just looks at him. Bengt and Knox and Reznikoff and Tlingit come out too, following Henrick, even Ojeira, who's kind of hop-walking, but he looks better doing it than he did before. They all stare at Luttinger. He was a big guy, strong, and he looks like very little right now.

"What the fuck," Bengt says. "They fucking ate him?"

I'm wishing I spoke the language, or understood the rules, but it isn't complicated, they want us dead, or gone. I look at him again. I add him up, the pieces. He's all this way and that but he's all there, just scattered.

"They weren't eating him," I say. "They were just killing him, I think." They all look at me. I nod to the snow, around us.

"They pissed all over this place. They mean to have it," I say. "They don't want us here. We don't belong here. That's all."

A wolf can kill a bear or a mountain lion, if he doesn't want them around, if they're too near his den. He won't eat those either, he just doesn't want them around. We've offended them, or scared them, or they don't like our smell, and they're going to correct the matter. When my father was young he was a deputy one winter he needed the money, in a town on the coast, before he found his calling slaughtering things. He walked into a bar with his gun on and his badge on his stupid hat like a 'shoot me' sign, he said, and guys jumped up and chairs went over, a bunch of guys thought he was there to get them, they came off a stolen boat full of stolen shit, whatever it was, and guns came out and he killed three of them, downed the other two and took four bullets himself and lived.

People would ask him how he lived through that. "Bullets go through me," he'd say. A secret of survival, he'd say, was not coming at anything sideways unless you knew you were doing it. He gave lessons in survival of all kinds. So I pissed off the wolves like that, or scared them like he did the guys in the bar. So now it's going to be to the death possibly, a conversation consisting of killing us all until the last word is dead on the snow. That's what they'd do if another pack of wolves wandered in. Maybe that's what they're doing.

I look out around us again. I know we have to move now but thinking feels slow in the cold. Thoughts are slowing and freezing, and the dead are slowing me down too instead of making me quicker, as they should. I look down at Luttinger, which has no point to it. I look out again looking for a line across the snow, whatever feels like west.

But I look to where we dragged the wood from, again, and out where the snow's blowing thick I think I see blur-lines moving through the snow. Wolves maybe. Or nothing. I keep watching, wait. The others see me looking, they start staring, dead-still, like the night before. I try to look through the snow until finally I figure they're faded back. Or were never there.

"What?" Henrick says. "You see something?" I shrug, and nod, which means maybe, or not.

"Anybody else see anything?" I ask.

Nobody did. We all stare though. They were there. Or never there. Brother ghosts. Brothers of the dead. Ghost walkers. Henrick looks at the snow where they marked, the paw-prints, the size of them, back at Luttinger.

"What do we do now?" he asks.

"Same as before. Get the fuck out." Ojeira looks from Luttinger across the clearing.

"Maybe we should stay here," Ojeira says. Knox nods.

"Yeah," Knox says. They both look scared.

"They mean to have it," I say again. "Get anything worth taking, and go." I say it in a way they'll understand we're in a hurry now, but I don't need to. They're scared for real, and nobody's arguing more for staying here, everybody's moving.

We start pulling together the stuff we've gathered the night before, but now we're rushing. I'm finding I like the daylight, what little is left. I find a knife that must have come out of somebody's bag. Half the guys at the camp wear knives on their belts like they're going to need to skin a deer before dinner. Henrick sees me pack the knife and he starts looking for one, and suddenly everybody thinks it's a good idea to have one, rush or not.

We look in the split scattered bags and all the loose crap around trying to find more, we get three more, a buck knife, a couple of silly little jack-knives. We take them all, not enough for all of us but still. Feeny gets up, holding his stump up, and finds the biggest, most asinine Bowie out in the snow wrapped up in somebody's long-johns. It's half a machete, and one hand or not he takes that for himself.

We find some backpacks we dump out, and a little more food than we found in the dark. Feeny finds a couple more lighters. We go through loose clothes and pockets of the dead for more. We find

51

a few phones we take in case they suddenly start working, for telling us where we are, or calling the ambulance we wanted. Or a taxi.

Tlingit finds a tray full of mini-bottles they must have had locked on board somewhere, because there's no booze on the north-bound plane bar or no bar. He stuffs his pockets with those, which hurry or not at that moment seems pretty sensible. Then he sits down on the snow a minute sampling them, which makes just as much sense. I'm tempted to sit there with him until they're all down between us. But, daylight. Bengt sees him.

"Tlingit. Come on," he says. Tlingit digs in his pocket and throws a bottle to Bengt, then more to the others, me too. I raise my bottle. To the dead, I suppose, and to us left.

"Fuck it," I say, and drink it.

"Fuck it," everybody else says, and drinks theirs. It's as good a prayer as any.

Henrick heads over to the dead fire where there's unburned wood left. He takes a ball-bat sized branch like the one he and Tlingit swatted the wolves off me with. He shoves it in his pack. That looks like a good idea. I go and get one too. Tlingit and the others find the best pieces they can.

We're more or less ready. Henrick looks at Luttinger, and out at the snow, then me.

"What if they come at us?" Henrick asks.

"Don't run. Can't outrun them. Stand your ground, try to look big. Better yet make noise, run at them with that stick, pray they'll think better of it."

Everybody looks at me, all of us hunching against the wind.

"If they get on one of us, do like you did for me. Gang up, swing at them. They don't want us here, but they don't care that much about us. Maybe if they see us heading out they won't come at us at all."

They look at me, skeptical again. I don't know if I believe what I'm telling them but I am trying to, it's what my head is telling me anyway. Bengt looks at me.

"Do you know what you're talking about or are you blowing air so we'll do whatever stupid thing you think we should do?"

"I know a little," I say. "And I'm blowing air."

"How do you know?" he asks.

I shrug. Doesn't matter how.

It feels like the day's waning already after twenty minutes. I look out to what I think is west or my best guess of it and it seems, as far as I can tell, to be a far enough direction away from any of the places we've seen wolves. I know that makes no difference but it makes me feel a little better.

So I look out to mark a point that might be west, in the line of trees on the far side of the clearing much further away than the ones we crashed through. At least I think it's west, and we haven't seen any wolves that way. I think wherever their den is, it's back in the trees where we gathered the wood, and we're lucky that west is the other way. If that's west.

"That way, okay?" I say. "Try to use the plane behind us as a mark, take a line across, okay?" Everybody nods, and we're about to set off when I see a wallet lying in the snow, and like an idiot I feel for mine, which is long gone. I didn't think of it till now.

"Lose something?" Tlingit seems to think it's funny.

I shrug.

"My wallet," I say, and he laughs.

Like I'll be needing it to get a drink somewhere. I shrug again. Nothing much in it that should matter to me, true enough. But not nothing.

I pick up the one in the snow and look at it, his license, no idea who the guy is, who it belongs to, smiling like a goon and dead, somewhere around here, or fell out of the sky miles away.

His wife and kids are in there, smiling, and I wonder if they're on hold with the company while the company gets ready to tell them they will be sure to find him or his remains very soon and that pension benefits, which will cover a trip to the grocery store, will be paid promptly. I look at his kids.

I want to get out of here but I go back over to the dead we brought out and reach and roll, looking to see if anybody has wallets, Lewenden, Luttinger, the rest. I throw them in a pile, and I check the other dead I can get to also. Henrick comes over. He and the others stare at me like I'm a lunatic.

"We should take them," I say. "For the families."

They all nod, suddenly. Henrick takes off his backpack, stuffs the wallets in. It's foolish, with so many we haven't gotten, but we do it anyway. We find ourselves looking at the bodies.

Henrick wants to have a service for them, say something, at least. They're all frozen stiff by now, and we've turned them all this way and that for knives and cell phones and satellite phones and now their wallets.

"Should we cover them over, at least?" Henrick says. I don't want to. I don't feel good staying another minute, I feel stupid enough taking the wallets. The light looks weaker.

"The snow will do it," I say.

Henrick looks at the ones we brought out and the rest, all we can see, Lewenden, the others, and the ones we can't, I suppose.

"God bless everyone who died here," he says. "Us too."

He stops, doesn't know what else to say. But we've sent them off as well as we're going to, and now there's us. I see we're standing there looking at each other.

I pull my bag over my shoulder on my good side and turn to the trees.

5

THE CLEARING IS bigger than it seemed. We've been walking a long time. We can barely see the plane behind us anymore, we've as good as lost it as a mark. But somehow the trees don't look any closer.

The daylight bled away before we even hit our stride, went to dusk, now it's hanging there between that and night again. We're out in the middle between what seems like the safety of the plane and the trees, feeling stranded, gone wrong already. Ojeira and Feeny have struggling to keep up, falling behind.

"Should we stop? Make a fire?" Henrick asks.

I don't know. I look at the trees, try to guess how far. And the wind is getting up even more than the morning, so I don't know if we could, and all we have to burn is the wood we took for clubs.

"We should keep on, if we can," I say.

"How much further are the fucking trees?" Bengt says. As if when we're in the trees we're home free.

"I don't know. I misjudged the distance." Bengt looks at me like I'm a tour-guide who doesn't know his job.

"That's fucking great. So we're out here for the night?" Bengt says. It's all night, more or less, from here. And the trees aren't going to save us from wolves, if they want us. But I don't say anything to him. I keep looking back to where I think the plane is, along our tracks, and Ojeira and Feeny trailing behind.

Ojeira's behind Feeny at the back, hobbling pretty bad. But he's still going better than he was before. I think maybe he's not as bad off as he seemed, even with his hernia or whatever it is. He didn't want us to help him like Luttinger and I did before. Maybe he's mending already. Feeny's only got the missing hand, but he might have fever or something, he's wobbling, walking drunken, it looks like. Maybe it's shock or loss of blood. He looks worse than Ojeira. The snow's hip-deep in places so none of us are going that fast, and they haven't dropped behind too badly. But they will before long.

"We should wait a little for those two, though," I say.

The others look back, waiting. After a minute Tlingit and some of them sit, breathing hard. We look around, again and again. I know we're looking for the wolves that are supposedly going to leave us alone and not bother us because we think we're trying to respectfully go the fuck home.

Ojeira and Feeny barely seem to be getting any closer, and Feeny keeps stopping to hold his stump up high. I think it's hurting whenever any blood fills into it so he gives up and walks with his hand in the air like he's on strike for something. We should have stopped sooner. As I look again Feeny looks like he's strung further back than Ojeira. The wind is creeping up harder, getting to be a slam. I stare back at them, in the half-light that's left, waiting for them. I wish they'd hurry.

Then, like before, I see something I'm not sure I'm seeing at all, lines moving in the dark, grey or black, two from the right, two from the left, one from behind, coming at Feeny. They don't seem interested in Ojeira. They've chosen Feeny, like they choose any animal, based on some invisible thing, and that's going to be that.

I start running before the others see them. I start straight for Feeny. But then I shift, head for the one of them coming from the right, the one closest it looks like, waving my arms, shouting. I hear the others doing the same, behind me, same as they did to beat that one off of me. We're far away. Feeny looks at us, sees us running, looks around. He sees the one from the right I'm charging at but he doesn't see the ones from behind him, or the left.

Ojeira looks too, almost falls backwards but catches his balance, stands there, frozen, then he starts jump-hobbling as hard as he can to help Feeny, yelling like the rest of us, but all they seem to care about is Feeny. They don't even care about me, so I yell louder and wave my arms. I realize there's a log and a knife in my pack and I'm empty-handed, running at them, but there's no time.

The one I'm charging at finally turns off Feeny to start at me, and the ones from behind and the left are still on Feeny but further from him, so I've gained him ten seconds maybe, or five, and now I have to keep charging at the one I've committed to.

"*Get on the others! Go!*" I yell back at the guys.

I seem to think there's some way if we split them up and charge at them we'll be able to get the others off Feeny. What we do with whichever wolves we pull off I don't know, but they'll be off Feeny. But run as hard as we can, and whether one of them is turned at me or not, I'm seeing we're far, further than I thought, and all the other black lines moving on Feeny are closer than we are. We can yell as loud as we want, but they aren't getting pulled off by us or anything.

Ojeira falls over in the snow and is yelling in pain. Then he's stumbling and tripping trying to get his feet back up on the snow, and he stumbles backwards when he sees them closing on Feeny. Then he stops, like he doesn't want to leave Feeny, but he can't make himself go get him. Neither would I. I'm still making for Feeny as fast as I can, but Feeny doesn't have any fight in him, and one of them hits Feeny. Then the lines all rush suddenly, faster than before, shoot at him like knives across the snow. They're all on him. The one I thought I pulled away turns and runs back at him too. I can't see Feeny any more at all under their bodies but I'm still trying to get to him, and yelling, but I realize I'm not aware of the others anymore behind me and they aren't yelling anymore, just me, and I realize I hear just Henrick.

"*Wait!*" Henrick's yelling. "*To your side!*"

I look around, and I see why he's yelling. The big wolf is there, running in at me, I never saw him at all, and he's much closer to me than the others, charging at me, cutting me off. I stop dead, involuntary, from fear. I just stop and look at him, and he stops too, our breath misting.

In the half-minute gone by it's almost full dark, as good as. But I'm closer to this one than I was when I saw him at the fire. I see him better than before. He's bigger than I thought. His hackles are up, his fur is darker, yellow-gold in his eyes. My muscles freeze. I feel them clenching by themselves, however the body arranges it so you feel fear, all of that is seizing up, my blood's trying to get out of me. And feeling all that I'm forced to notice he's a beautiful kind of thing. He looks like death to me, which is not the thought I want in my head.

A couple of the other wolves trot up from nowhere to his flanks, out of the dark. They stand there, stare at me too, stopping me or anybody else from getting to Feeny. Then I'm aware we're all strung out staring at the ones in front while Feeny is getting dragged this way and that in the snow by the others, and I can't hear him. He's quiet by now, or not making any noise loud enough to hear from here, and the big one and the ones with him keep staring at me, daring me to go at them.

So like an idiot I do. I go in at them, thinking of Feeny. I pull off my pack and run in at the big one roaring and swinging the pack at him, with the log inside, and he barely blinks. He and the others just hop out of my way, loop around me again, and seeing I'm past them I charge on for Feeny a few steps but I feel them coming up behind.

I turn, face them. Now I'm between two sets of wolves, away from the other guys, and I'm fucked. I can't go to Feeny because the big one and the others will run me down from behind if I do, and if I charge him again he'll just do what he did again. He's outplayed me.

I look at him and the two on his flanks while they loop around in front of me again, between me and Feeny, daring me in the same stupid game. I'm beaten. I just watch while Feeny is pulled and ripped, and the others watch too, I don't know how long. Not long and too long. Feeny's dead, probably.

The first wolves who hit him are walking away from him. Then one by one the others stop and stroll away, until the smallest one seems to realize he's the last. He finally stands up and walks away, too, and we see Feeny's a dark mess in the snow. It's hard to see what there is of him. There was no sitting with him helping him over or telling him he's going to die. I just let him get ripped apart and watched it.

The wolves have taken up this circle looking at us now, not moving, waiting for us to comprehend. We see Ojeira standing off looking at Feeny, terrified. The wolves look at us like somebody who's just hit you and is waiting to see if you got the point, if you're going to try and get up again or if you understand now who just hit you, and how hard.

The big one stares at me, more fixed than any of the others, who keep glancing over at him. He doesn't look like something I could shake off my back. He looks more like he'd go through my back on the way to my stomach and cut me in half. I stare at them, afraid to do anything, waiting.

Then he gets off his paws and charges me, straight over the snow, not taking his eyes off me. I'm still out in front, I don't know how many yards ahead of the others, but enough to feel alone. I don't think I can laugh my way through another fight with a wolf, not this one. I watch him coming, and I tighten up, can't help it. I know this wolf can kill me, if he decides he wants to, but I'm too scared to run away and too scared to run at him, I don't know what to do.

I watch him come at me, closer and closer, twenty feet, fifteen, and I'm afraid to move or I know I'm dead if I do, and he just stops dead, ten feet away, staring at me. I still don't move. I remember other wolves I've had staring matches with, and I've never seen one look at me like this. This one hates every winter he's ever had, and hates the fifty blood brawls he's fought because he's the biggest, and the meanest, and he's had to. I'm here, now, in his place. He might hate me too, and anybody with me. Watching him, I feel like he's still deciding what he's going to do with us.

He sits down, calmly, and I still don't move. None of the others do either I don't think. I can't hear anything behind me. I don't know if they're still there and I'm afraid to look. Then he stands again, forward on his paws, and he shoots straight at me another few feet again and stops dead again and stares at me, and snarls again, and I stay still, again.

With him this much closer I can feel him jumping on me, but he doesn't jump yet. He's close enough for him to jump at me if he wants, but not close enough for me to reach out and grab him, or swing at him, if I was that brave. I don't like him being smarter than me and he is, out here. Maybe my father hated them because they were smarter than him.

I shift a little, in my boots. I don't mean to. It's hard to stay as still as I've been trying to. It looks like I'm leaning forward, a piece of an inch, at most. He bares his teeth, his lips peeled back, ears down, tail in the air, straight up, brushing back and forth. He keeps his eyes on mine and snarls again, from the bottom of somewhere I never want to be. His teeth are huge, all out of his mouth for show, and he's telling me: 'Get out of my house, you piece of shit.'

We keep staring at each other in the wind. I don't know what to do but stare. Then he turns, circles around, so he'll see me if I come at him. But I don't go at him, and he trots off and leaves me there. He lopes past Feeny and Ojeira toward the dark and they all fall in behind him, loping away. I'm finally brave enough to turn my head and see Henrick and the others, behind me. The big wolf turns again, looks back at us, from farther off. One of the ones next to him starts to howl, and the others join in, and the big one tilts back and howls too.

I still don't move. None of us does. We just stand there listening to them howling, watching, then they string out and fade into the dark one by one, and we can't see them at all, just hear them howling, till the last one finally stops.

Then we don't know where they are anymore, after a few seconds. They might have looped around and come next to us, in the dark, by now. I look around at Henrick and the others and I listen for paws in the snow, their breath, a yelp, but there's nothing.

The wind shifts hard, like a door slamming. As cold as it is, I think I smell them, the smell they left behind. I look back to the trees where we were heading before the wolves came after Feeny, where we imagine west is, but don't know. At least the wolves went something like the other way, back behind us, which is something, I suppose. Bearings are hard to hold. I don't know if the trees we were trying to head for are the ones I'm looking at now. I know very little but cold.

I start back to Feeny to see if he's alive, which seems insane to me, because that's the direction the wolves went into the dark, but I start back for him anyway, and besides Ojeira is sitting there, looking stranded. The others don't move at first, then they follow me. We want to stick together. We're watching and listening, all the time, and it's hard going back, but we get to Ojeira, who's getting himself up. He's shaking, because he was closer.

"Are you okay?" I ask him. He nods, terrified and disgusted at the same time.

We keep on a little further, snow blowing at us, and get to Feeny. I see ribs and meat. He looks like a deer you're dressing to lay in a deep-freeze, and my skin and my muscles creep, seeing him. It's worse than Luttinger looked, somehow.

I look around in the dark, and I still can't see the wolves though I know they might be standing there, waiting. But they seem to be gone for the minute, watching us maybe, I don't know. I bend down over him, reach under the mess. The snow blowing stings my hands and I feel the warmth coming off Feeny's carcass, but I still reach under him.

"What the hell are you doing?" Henrick says.

I'm after Feeny's wallet. Why I think he'd still have it I don't know, blood's everywhere and hacks of flesh and it isn't something I'm enjoying. But I find it, to my surprise, half in his pocket, half in the snow. Henrick starts scooping up snow with his bare hands, covering him, and Tlingit and Bengt and Knox help, me too. It seems the least we can do, what we didn't do for the others. Maybe it's for us more than for him. We do a little, and I know the snow will cover him soon anyway for winter, and after won't matter.

Tlingit picks up Feeny's pack, which is lying a few feet away. He reaches in and takes out Feeny's knife, and a couple of bags of peanuts, and the lighters Feeny found. He stuffs the peanuts in his pack and keeps the knife in his hand. I pull my pack off and get my knife out too, put it in my pocket, and the piece of wood I have. I feel two kinds of idiot for not having them ready before. Everybody else does the same. It was probably stupid to come and stand over him like this. More than probably.

We head for the trees again. All of us look around every step now. I'm thinking if they hit Feeny because he was straggling, walking drunk like he was, then they're still watching us, waiting to choose another. Probably Ojeira, I think. I look at him, and feel bad for thinking it.

As sure as I am they're watching us, I'm hoping that, somewhere in my head, they're seeing us going, they've shown us enough, and they're satisfied. But I don't know. The clearing seems to go on forever, we walk and walk, fast as we can manage, staring at the strip of forest, making up the ground we lost going back for Feeny, and slogging on, waiting every step for something else to come out of the dark, take another one of us. Sometimes they want the weakest, if they're hunting, and sometimes the strongest, if they're fighting. I try to act like neither, which is as good as saying: '*Take that other fucker, don't take me.*' But it's an old habit, keeping my head down. I tell myself if they don't jump me, better for me to save whoever they do jump. That's what I tell myself.

I watch the line of trees bobbing up and down in the distance between the snow and the sky. We all seem to think we'll be safer in the trees. I know we won't be, but you get driven by these feelings whether they make any sense or not. I look ahead, tying to measure how far we have to go.

The trees look like a black shore with more dark behind it, like the edge of the world, and somehow after hours of not seeming any closer we seem to be getting to the point where it's enlarging, and the darkness of the trees we've been praying to reach starts to open up, bit by bit. It seems close finally. Not so much that we start to ease, but it seems closer.

But suddenly they come out of the dark, again, just like that, they're there, the big one and the others, they were there all along, keeping pace with us, but they step in close enough for us to see them, now. They start to circle, far out to our right and left, watching us, and then I see more behind us, on our flank.

We're all scared, standing there, staring. Reznikoff just starts running for the trees, like a maniac. It's one kind of chance if you're crazy enough to run toward them but it's no chance at all if you run when they're behind you. They'll run you down like caribou.

"*Don't run!*" I yell out. "*Don't fucking run!*"

But Reznikoff isn't listening. Henrick's ahead of me and he starts trying to run him down before the wolves do. I charge after Henrick a few steps and stop, yelling '*Don't!*'

But Henrick keeps going, so now both of them are running for the trees while the wolves are just watching, straining to go, it looks like. They keep looking at the big one to see what he'll do, and the rest of the guys back with me are, I can tell, straining to take off too rather than get left back here, but I keep saying, "Don't move, let Henrick get him."

Then I see the wolves start, just like that. I don't see any signal or anything from the big one, they just begin, shooting across at Henrick and Reznikoff, and then we're committed.

I take off after Henrick, running as hard as I can, piece of wood in my hand, roaring again, because I know it's insane and because if I make enough noise maybe we'll be lucky, and the ones behind me won't close the distance before I can somehow get the ones in front of me off Reznikoff and Henrick, and somehow get us all on one side of them so we can face them, instead of being tied up in a bag like we are now.

I can see four wolves, now six, now more, and all of them seem to have a bead on Reznikoff, and it looks like Henrick too, hard to see from the angle, running like I am. I know Reznikoff has seen them, but he's committed, and he's committed the rest of us now too, so here we fucking go. I'm hauling as fast as I can.

The rest of the guys are running behind me, we want into those trees as silly as that is, so we might as well run as fast as we can, right into the wolves, if we can. Maybe two more of us will live to die later of hunger, or later tonight when the wolves come after us again.

Reznikoff's way ahead of us. Henrick too, but he's not as fast as Reznikoff. Reznikoff's way ahead of us. It looked like he maybe had a hundred yards to run into the trees and he must have run fifty by now. I look at the wolves closing on him and the distance we have to go compared to the distance they have to go. Suddenly they're closing on him faster and Henrick and I are still charging but it doesn't matter, or isn't going to.

Reznikoff twists back and looks at the wolves closing on him, and he seems to know. There are a lot of them now, maybe all of them, eight, ten, they're springing out of the back of the dark, and I see the big one loping, in no rush. As I'm running trying to catch them the one in front doubles his speed, shoots away from the pack, straight at Reznikoff and into him. I don't see a jump or a leap, he just shoots into him. Three more of them rush in too, then others. Henrick falters and stops. So do I.

The big wolf doesn't rush in, he watches. He looks at us, and the wolves that haven't rushed in at Reznikoff stop and look at us too.

Reznikoff's standing, somehow. He was down but he's up again, covered in wolves hanging on him like they did on me. He looks so far away, and I see him twisting left and right and then he goes down like I did. He disappears under the wolves.

Henrick and I and the others stand and watch. It's a soul-damning time, longer than Feeny. Long enough to go to hell in. We're stuck, or hypnotized, but I can't move, suddenly, can't charge them, not now. None of us can, this time. There are too many, we're too afraid, they'll just go behind us like they did when I tried to get to Feeny. Whatever stopped us, we stopped.

When I think I can't stand it anymore I look across to open snow away from the wolves and Reznikoff and away from where we were heading, and I look at Henrick and we think the same thing, I think, the others too.

"Leave him," I say. But I've yelled it. I wonder if Reznikoff heard it.

Henrick hesitates a second. Tlingit too. After that we're all running for the trees as hard as we can, after all my speeches and yelling about not running. I want to get into the trees before they leave Reznikoff and hit us. I barely look to see if the other wolves are chasing us and they aren't, maybe they know they don't need to.

We run and try not to think of Reznikoff, and we think we're getting away with something, God help us. We're coming closer to the trees, but we're not there. I look back as I run and I know Ojeira will be in the back and he is, he can't run any better than that jump-hop hobble he was doing before. I keep looking back to see if they're coming for him. By miracle or by something they don't.

The trees finally loom up big and I stop and let the others run in and look back for the wolves and for Ojeira who is somehow in his awful way doing a decent speed now. Why they haven't picked him off I don't understand but he jump-hops up with me, and we run the last part together, then somehow we're in the trees. We pass in to the bottom-of-the-world darkness.

Not far in at all, we all stop short, panting. We look out to the clearing. I can't see them or Reznikoff, or anything but snow and dark. We back away, still looking, and as we feel the slope drop under us we turn away finally and stumble and run down the snowdrifts as fast as we can, as if further into dark is safer. We've run into the dark like ghosts, left our bodies behind.

We blunder in the dark, barely missing trees we only see once they're right in front of us that we stiff-arm to keep from smashing into. We keep running into even deeper dark, moon is gone. We're huffing and puffing, trying not to think about Reznikoff and Feeny. We're wondering where the wolves are.

I can barely see anything, or any of the guys. I look ahead and I see patches where a little moonlight is coming down, some ways off. But here the ground in front of us is black and blank. I can hear us breathing. I look up the slope behind us to see, or try to hear if any of the wolves are coming in behind us, as if I could hear them.

The wind is blunted in here. But trees creak and crack, hum, and it's almost worse. Everything sounds like wolf. But for all I listen, there's nothing. Only dark and the air washing through the trees.

I don't want to stay here. I run-stumble on again, still headlong, still huffing, thinking if I step into a ravine and smash to pieces I'll be home-free and thank God, I've decided the matter, and hopefully the others will notice before they fall in after me. I keep rushing on blind, one arm in front and trying to see anything at all, and I ram into branches and trunks and fall into holes, and haul and haul on.

6

WE ALL STOP again, closer to where the patches of moon are coming down. We're wheezing, aching, half-pissing ourselves, leaning on trees, looking back to what seems like where we came from and all around us, because we don't know if they're in here with us yet, or coming. There's some glow too, I see, not just patches of light, and I see the slope shallowing out. It rolls down below us, with trees reaching up and dark above, it stretches ahead like a vast cave. I stare into it. Cathedral trees, leviathan, a maze of them, dead giants at their feet, lightning-struck or fallen from age, roots-up, naked, massive.

Maybe the wolves are in here with us. Maybe new ones, a dozen or a hundred lined up around us, watching, blinking, unhappy with us. We've seen I suppose ten at most. It's been hard to count them. Seems like not many more than that, maybe only eight. Enough, though.

We make our way forward, or what we think is forward, through the maze of dead and fallen trees. We've slowed down, not because we think it's smart, but because we're exhausted and like fools, we think we've made some division between the open of the clearing and this place, as if the wolves couldn't follow us in and be three feet beyond what we can see, laughing at our blindness.

I'm praying I can keep some idea of which way anything is in here. I tell myself I'm still taking a line that's something like west, what we decided was west, anyway. But I don't know at all if that's the case, or if we'll go in circles until we die, and the wolves will watch us and laugh again, or get tired of waiting and go on tearing us to pieces one by one.

We keep on, a good ways down until the slope drops even steeper and it looks like it bottoms out, to what I don't know. The floor of the place, if it has a floor. I want the shape of things to make sense as if that will let me grapple better in the dark, but if it were full daylight I doubt I'd do much more than fumble ahead, now. The wind is still coming but not as fierce, and in all the bumps and twists and turns of snow and rock and trees and blind gullies I think I hear water somewhere. I do hear something that isn't wind off to our side or ahead of us, or somewhere. Sounds get lost in the snow like we've gotten lost. But I think there's water running, a little piece of river or a biggish stream. I think if we could find a real river, it might take us to the coast, and we could follow the coast to a town and live. It's a nice thought.

I lose the sound anyway. All I hear is wind coming up harder, washing the trees again and I wonder if that's all I ever heard. Washing us away particle by particle. My brain's too cold again, or the air is too thin for thinking.

I don't know how high in the mountains we are. For all I know we've been in thin air all this time, thinking worse and worse the more hours we breathe it. We should get used to it. I remember crossing mountains and getting used to it, having thoughts run away and being out of breath and feeling your heart float off in front of you, and day by day getting stronger and having all that come back to me. But I don't know that we're fit to get used to

IAN MACKENZIE JEFFERS

anything. Maybe if you're bleeding, or half-dead to start with, you don't get better, you get worse, you drift off like molecules, like puffs of breath, until you aren't there anymore. I keep going, listening, still, trying to catch the sound again and follow it, but it's blown away from me like I've blown away from myself. If there was ever any sound of any river. There's nothing now again, hopes or no hopes, but wind, and us stumbling and crunching in the snow, huffing like cattle.

I walk on, because that's all we can do. I'm almost sure I hear it again. I stop again, try to listen, everybody else stops too. Scared as we are, we're ready to stop anytime. We forget the wolves, occupied with the business of putting one boot in front of the last. It's tired and cold we care about now, if no wolf's right in front of us, teeth out. Lazy, stupid beasts, we are. It makes me think we don't deserve to live this out. That they deserve to live more. But I don't think the fools with me deserve to die.

I listen, try not to breathe. But the sound's gone again. I stand there waiting for the wind to bring it back or my brain to catch it again, trying to listen through my breathing and everyone else's. I can't see them, except Henrick and Tlingit, barely, but I hear them. I hope it's all of us, I don't know.

The wind shifts. I think I smell them again, the wolves, and my skin pricks. Then I think I couldn't be smelling them. It's dead wood or wet bark or frozen mud, or my wounds rotting. Or it's the general stink of us, fear, the dirt we brought with us. I stand there until I give up on the river or my hallucination of the river, and walk on.

Nobody talks. We grunt as we haul out of deep snow or over trees or stumble into things. For the last five minutes of going everyone's been falling and tripping in the snow and pulling themselves up again. I want to rest. If it kills me I don't care.

72

"We should stop," I whisper out to Henrick and the others. I don't know why I bother to whisper, or don't mean to, it just comes out a whisper.

Henrick and Tlingit and Knox drop packs, their pieces of wood, collapse in the snow. I think I hear the others do the same.

"Who sees the others?" I say to Henrick.

"We're here," Bengt says. I hear them clamber through the snow, come in closer, wheezing. Then I see everybody, Knox and Ojeira. We've slowed down so much in here Ojeira's kept up with us. They drop their packs again, collapse again, everybody still wheezing and puffing. It makes me feel better to see us all. Mother hen. I don't want to lose anyone else.

We sit there, catching breath, or trying to, looking around in the dark.

"You think they're in here?" Tlingit says. I look around us.

"I don't know," I say.

We're freezing, but we're afraid to build a fire, in case it tells them where we are. We'd rather stay in the dark and freeze. We're all more exhausted than before, and more scared than before, after Reznikoff and Feeny.

"We just fucking left him," Bengt says. "I fucking ran."

"We all did. We left Feeny too," Henrick says. He's trying to make less of it. He's looking at Bengt like Bengt should forgive himself.

"Yeah, Feeny too. Fucking left them," Bengt says, shaking his head. "Fucking watched."

Nobody wants to argue. We're too scared. It will occupy your mind. It's true what they say, about death, if you think it's behind you about to lay a hand on you.

Afraid or not, I know we'll freeze sitting here. After a minute I get up, start pulling branches off a downed tree. They're long dead, they snap when I pull them, dry but rotted. They'll burn, once they start, flare up fast, but won't last long.

I toss them in a pile with some smaller pieces and more solid ones and feel for the lighter in my jacket. I realize my hands feel like they died a long time ago too, they're like pieces of meat. But I can feel the little lighter in my pocket and I fumble for a good half-minute trying to get it out, then another trying to light it under a little bundle of twigs, but the wind is still sucking everything away.

"We want to do that?" Henrick asks.

"They know where we are," I say, because I've known that all along, whatever I thought. "If they want to, they do."

Finally I get a little flame out of the lighter and I shelter the lighter and the twigs down by Henrick and Knox. They hunch over to block the wind the best they can, but nothing's catching. Tlingit steps in too, and I hold the little bit of there-and-gone flame to the smaller pieces and I'm happy when they start to catch.

I get the pieces down without them blowing out and lay the bigger dry rotted ones on and it starts to go, fluttering sideways looking like it's blowing out on and off but going. Then the heat's stronger than the wind is, the bigger pieces finally catch and it's up. Henrick and Tlingit and Ojeira stand in close, me too.

I keep looking between the branches and the trunks around us, into the dark. I look as deep into it as I can, the firelight behind me, but I don't see anything. Out at the edges there are things that might be shaggy broken pieces of tree or might be wolves. Everything looks like wolves, like everything sounded like wolves before. I keep staring to see if I can get some clue, or catch them moving, but all the dark lumps and clumps seem to be only that. To my surprise I feel myself ease, which is foolish.

With the fire going I hunch as close as I can to it. We all do. Then I look to some thinner branches scattered, some on the ground some on the trees, and I get myself up and start gathering all I can, cutting the ones I have to with my knife and snapping when I can or twisting them when I can't, some greener than others. I leave the rotten ones, they turn to dust. I get a good few of them and sit down by the fire with the others still getting warm, with my knife, and start trimming off the smallest twigs until I have a shaft, and then I start shaving a point on it. It's still green, it bends more than I'd hoped, but I think it will work.

The others see what I'm doing and haul themselves up to do the same, scattering out to find branches we can use, except Ojeira, who just sits, and nobody blames him. I hold the point of mine in the fire, turning it until it's black, pulling it out if it catches and dousing it in the snow or with my hand, or blowing it out. I'm thinking it hardens the point if you char it. Might, anyway. I roll it a last few times in the flame and pull it out and the tip is glowing, smoking wisps and I hope harder now. Not as green at least. I give Ojeira the first one I've done and start on the next.

The others have come back to the fire by now and sit and fumble their knives with close to useless hands, and start carving and scraping. We all sit there whittling and looking around us once in a while in the wind. I want to make as many as I can. They aren't so heavy, I think I could carry a bundle of them with me, along with the log and a knife, and stand off this pack and almost everybody else who's ever bothered me.

The fire starts to bulk upward, thicker yellow-orange, and I see the wind is dropping, just like that, blowing off somewhere else, leaving us here. The sound of it fades away and it's strange, the emptiness of the air all of a sudden. I listen again for whatever I thought was the sound of water running, but I can't hear it. Maybe I never did.

"These going to do anything?" Ojeira asks. I shrug again.

"I don't know," I say. "Might not matter."

"What does that mean?" Henrick says.

"Means it might not matter."

"Why? Because we're fucked anyway?"

"Does it matter to you?" I say. "If a wolf gets you or we freeze?"

"Yeah, it fucking matters. I've got a baby girl. I want to go home."

"Okay," I say. "Of course you do."

"You fucking have kids?" Henrick says. He's gotten angry. I don't say anything. Not for me to say.

"Well I fucking do, and I want to get home," he says. "You don't know, you don't have kids, you don't know shit." Tlingit and Bengt and the others stare at Henrick and me.

"I didn't say I didn't," I say. Henrick looks at me.

"I have a son," I say. "I don't see him, okay?" Henrick looks at me. He's still angry anyway.

"And it doesn't matter to you, if we get back? Why don't you let the next fucking wolf eat you then?"

I look at him, I nod to show he's right, and I don't want to fight. I go back to shaving the point. I shrug.

"Somebody's got to look after you babies," I say.

He looks at me sharp, shrugs, finally, still mad. *'Fine, if you're trying to get me home, fine, fuck you very much,'* he's thinking. *'We don't have to swap baby pictures.'* He goes back to shaving his stick. We aren't going to get up and kill each other. I don't feel good I upset him. He wants his little girl. I don't blame him.

We try to let the fire get into us, stomachs empty, wolves watching us, maybe, sniffing out their next, maybe, who gives a fuck. Fuck them.

"How old?" Tlingit says. He's looking at Henrick. Henrick looks at him, finally.

"She's two."

Tlingit nods.

"She cute?"

Henrick laughs, much as somebody can in what we're in. He nods.

"Yeah, she's my angel."

That's what everybody says about their little girls. But I've heard enough guys say that I know it's true. I see it, looking at him anyway, freezing to death, terrified, thinking of his baby girl. It's true, she is his angel, I know. He'd die for her.

I look at Henrick.

"She have a good laugh?" I say. "Your girl?"

Henrick smiles. He isn't angry at me as much now.

"She's got a fucking hilarious laugh," he says. "Your boy?"

"Fucking hilarious," I say. "First time he peed standing up he thought it was the funniest thing in the fucking world. Laughed his little ass off. Made us proud."

Henrick laughs, the others too. Tlingit looks at Knox.

"You have family?" he asks Knox.

"I got three," Knox says, and I see his eyes light, and then like Henrick he looks like a stone just got heavier. He's thinking about them, worrying he may not get home, by the odds. I put the spear I've sharpened into the fire, turn it.

"I've been trying, with my wife," Ojeira says. "When I'm down-shift."

77

"That's hard work there," Bengt says. Ojeira laughs.

"I'll take that over this," he says.

"Maybe you have one in the works then," Tlingit says.

Ojeira doesn't seem to have thought of it. His eyes brighten, then go empty, like Knox's did, and Henrick's.

"I tell her I hate her three times a week," he says. The others laugh. He's smiling, then he looks sorry he said it, and he sits there, thinking of her, more kindly than he sounded, it looks like. Bengt shakes his head.

"I got an ex-girlfriend who thinks I'm an asshole," he says. "And that I should marry her."

The guys laugh at that, again, little grunt laughs.

Tlingit looks at me, like he's waiting for me to say something. I look at my boots, then at the point I'm turning in the fire. It gets quiet again, wind gusting.

"Your boy with his mom?" Tlingit asks. He never asked me about my boy before, or my wife. Because I know how to have people not ask me things.

"He does," I say. "He's better off." I guess I say it in that way that sounds sorry for itself, or just sorry. Nobody wants to say anything more after that. It gets quiet again. We've probably told each other all we ever want to know about each other, and probably all we'll ever know. And we're too scared we'll never see anybody else again to talk any more anyway. We're too scared of everything, night, dying, pain. Maybe we'd be happy to be dead but we're afraid of the pain, and we're afraid of fear we can't strangle down like we've strangled down most of the other fears we've had to deal with, some of them, at least. So we're out of things to say, and we're thinking about the people who make us halfway human, and we're aching in our bones for them. And we all know that about each other or can guess it, and that sits in the air, the only thing that matters to us anymore. Everybody goes on carving, making shucking and squeaking sounds in the cold. I start cutting a point on another stick.

"You see though?" Henrick says, finally. "That's why you're alive. Your son."

I nod, looking at the point I'm carving.

"I'm alive because I'm lucky," I say.

I should have died in the plane, I think. Maybe I did, it's just taking some extra hours to conclude the business. Henrick looks at the fire.

"I don't fucking want to die here," he says. Nobody says anything. He looks at me.

"What do we do? If those wolves stay on us?" Henrick asks me. I'm quiet again. We all are.

"We try to fight them," I say. "If we have to. If they won't let us walk out. Stop them."

"How are we supposed to do that?" Ojeira says.

"One at a time. Tip the numbers," I say. I keep carving the point. "That's what they're doing to us."

I don't believe we have a hope in hell of winning a thing like that. But I want them to believe it. Maybe they won't come at us again. Maybe if they do we'll get lucky, fend them off, at least. I'm thinking about my wife and my son again. I try not to, but here they are, around the fire with me.

Before our son came, my wife had a dream about wolves. She dreamed that wolves took me, dragged me off in the snow somewhere. In the dream when she got to me I weighed nothing anymore, I was light and half-gone, and in the dream all she thought was *'But you haven't known our son.'* She sobbed and sobbed, in her sleep, as she dreamed, for me and our son. I used to pray to things. I've had my discussions, stumbling drunk, or facing a knife in an alley, looking at guns, the bad end. Hard times in cold houses, night walks I didn't bargain for, in the shadows of what the world doesn't think about, hunts that went wrong when for a moment of stupid a mountain has almost killed me, or a forest, because I was foolish. But I've found myself praying to the memory of that dream and what she told me, crying, later. I've prayed to the love of our son and me she had in her dream. Without her knowing, I suppose, that was God to her once, sleeping in the cave of her night. It was to me.

And now my son is across a curve of earth from here and I don't know what time it is. It's dinner, or he's going to bed without his father, and better off for it. If I get back alive, chances are better than not his life will be worse. I wonder if disappearing here might be as good a thing as I could give him. That's what I've tried to think, away from him, that I'm doing what's best. It's a hard thing to think every day. It's not nothing to choose that.

I look up at these babies making their spears. We've been making the silly little spears and having our fireside all-going-to-die-soon time. I wonder if it's enough that we could get up and move again. Stopping the night when it's nothing but night loses its meaning. Everybody sits, quiet, watching the dark and the fire by turns. I look at Ojeira, see him nodding, falling asleep, and Bengt looks the same. I feel myself slipping too.

I look up from the fire, suddenly, wondering if I've fallen asleep, and how long if I have. The fire's down, cold's crept into me. I see everyone's asleep. How we can fall asleep when a thousand yards back wolves were on us, I don't know. What do you do after watching people die? Eventually you'll sleep again, it'll come. But suddenly

I feel we've stayed too long. I knock my boots together in the snow to clean the treads, like that's going to matter after two steps. I haul myself to my feet, and reach to Henrick, shake him.

Henrick snaps awake, startled, looks around.

"I think we get moving, if we can," I say. Henrick nods, shakes Tlingit, who does the same, hauls up. The others wake up, too, see we're still here, and look unhappy. I pick up the sticks I sharpened, nod to the sticks we haven't sharpened yet.

"Let's bring those too," I say.

I pull my pack on, as the others get to their feet, except Ojeira, who's struggling. Henrick and I bend down to help him up, and I stop.

The wolves have come in by the fire, standing there, staring at us. Maybe they were here all the time we slept. I didn't hear them come, they're just there. Three, I see right away, and my heart's pounding wondering where the others are. Henrick sees me staring, looks, the others too. They're very close, at the edge of what's left of the firelight, looking at us. Nobody wants to move. I see more now I'm looking, four more, dotted between the trees, could be others. They're there somewhere.

"Shit. Shit," Ojeira says, whispering, still on the ground, fumbling for his knife, which he's dropped or something, he can't find it. He has his sticks but we all seem to want as many sharp things as we can have our hands on, not that we know what we're going to do. He's the only one moving, he keeps patting around in the snow trying to find his knife and finally he finds it behind him, he was almost sitting on it, and he half gets up and falls back down with it, point up, holding all his sticks up too.

"If they come at us, we fight them," I say, staring at the wolves in front. "If any of them gets on one of us, we gang on that one, okay?

Try to get a stick into him, or a knife, if you can." They're all staring, paralyzed, like that's the last thing they'll ever be able to do.

I keep looking for the big one, I don't see him. Finally he comes out of the dark, stands there, staring with the rest of them. I don't know what they're doing, sniffing us out, choosing one of us to kill or deciding to kill all of us at once, or just waiting to see what the big one does. I breathe, watch them breathing.

The big one straightens his body out, suddenly, leans forward, makes a line, nose to back, pointing at me, low. I think he's getting ready to come at me.

"What the fuck is he doing?" Ojeira says.

"I don't know," I say. "Choosing."

The big wolf looks from me to Ojeira, sniffing. Then he shifts, barely. He's pointing at Ojeira, now.

"Is he fucking looking at me? He's what— choosing me?"

I don't know what they're doing.

"If they hit you, we'll get them off you. You'll be okay." I know I'm lying, but we can try.

"You beat them away from me before, you can do it again," I say to Henrick and the others. Henrick and Tlingit stare at them.

Behind the big wolf, I see the other wolves lean in too, setting low, like the big one. They're all looking at Ojeira, it looks like, which is turning Ojeira into jelly, he's panting, shaking, starting to scrabble backwards.

"Stay put," I tell him.

"Oh Jesus. God, Jesus," he says.

Ojeira jumps, suddenly, flicks his eyes to a skinny wolf on his flank, gasping. I didn't see him before, but there he is, and Ojeira yelps and half-shoves backwards, looks the wolf in the eye. The wolf looks at Ojeira, takes a step closer, low, straight, like an arrow. I half-turn to be ready, but I can't turn too far or I'm show-ing my back to the others.

It doesn't matter. The wolf shoots in, rushes toward Ojeira. Ojeira screams, holds his knife and his spears up all at once, fum-bling. He's too scared to have any strength, but he's half-keeping the wolf at bay, it stops.

We wait another quarter-second and then the wolf shoots in the rest of the way to Ojeira, jumps him, and all the other wolves, all but the big one, run around us and past us, shoot in at Ojeira too. Ojeira's eyes go wide and his sticks scatter and fly and I grab up my stick and lay my knife along the shaft and I charge after them, hoping the big one doesn't charge up from behind again. Henrick and Tlingit and Bengt and Knox do the same. The wolves have all jumped on to Ojeira by now, they've put their backs to us, and none of them is turning on us or getting between us and Ojeira this time, either they've counted us out, or counted we were going to let them take Ojeira.

I've run a few steps closer. There's the one at Ojeira's middle but I have to get past the one closest who's got Ojeira's knee in his maw. I've started roaring, at some point, we're all roaring, sticks high, and I don't know how to go about this but I try to jump up over the one at Ojeira's knee and fall down at the flank of the one at Ojeira's middle with the point of the stick. Ojeira's scrabbling back trying to push him off.

The point catches, and I'm amazed to see it sink under his fur but then it slides right through, I've just poked in under his fur and now I've fallen in the snow and lost my knife. I look back, still down, scared, to see where the big one is and he's gone.

But the wolf I went at has noticed the stick, and me, and as I bang around in the snow for my knife and as Tlingit and Henrick and the others are roaring and swinging sticks and logs the wolf next to me twists and snarls and half-flips away from Ojeira to see what just bit him. I forget the knife and hold tighter on the stick that's still snagged in him and I try to get up.

He doesn't like it, but it isn't doing anything, either, and he sees me getting up off my knees and I yank the stick back out of him but I stumble back in the snow and I drop it, and he notices that too. He barks and hop-jumps half in the air and comes down on his forepaws and stares at me. He's off Ojeira, at least, and on me.

I grab for the stick and scramble back to my feet as I see Henrick ram his stick at the next one and hits its side, I think. But it twists and flips away under Henrick and backs up, looking at him like mine is looking at me, then it hops to the side and into the dark and we don't know where it is at all, running around to come at us another way, I think. All this at the same time as Knox looks to be wrestling with one and keeping it off him for the instant. I hear the others yelling and yelping barking yips but I can't see everybody. Tlingit's out of sight, Bengt too.

More wolves have jumped in at Ojeira. Henrick tries to get them off him, and I face mine, wondering if I'll live if I charge it or he'll swipe me in half. As I'm deciding if I can charge I hear them running, somewhere around us.

I think I see blurs in the dark, dark in dark again. But I have mine to think about. He's blocking the way between me and the wolves on Ojeira. I see Tlingit fall backwards out of the dark and scrabble back to his feet looking back into dark at whatever he was facing, but he's got a log in his hands and he sees Ojeira and he turns to help Henrick, swinging and swinging his piece of wood at the wolves at Ojeira with all his might and barely getting their attention. Then I see Bengt has been there all along but he's down, for some reason, beating and poking at the wolves on Ojeira without bothering to stand. They've been on Ojeira too long.

I finally go in at mine. He dodges me, scurries like the big one did before. Then he stands off, watching me, and I give up on him. I pray he won't run me down and I run to help Bengt and Tlingit and Henrick get the others off Ojeira while Ojeira's screaming, trying to shove the ones closest to his neck off him. But my wolf does run me down, I turn just as it's on me and about to get his teeth on my legs and I roar at it and try to tower up big and drive at it with the stick and all I do is poke him again. He twists away like he's nothing but air and jumps back, watching.

I chance leaving him again and turn to Ojeira and I see a wolf pushing close to his neck no matter how much the others are pounding and poking and pulling at it, and not knowing what else to do I shove in at him and grab him under his belly like I'm picking up a puppy and pull him backwards off Ojeira, and I fall backwards with his weight. He turns to snap at me and still falling backwards I spin and throw him off me into the snow, but I as good as run into the one I left to run in at this one. He lands on him instead, and falls into the snow, and they both hop back up barking at us.

I look for the big one again. I finally see some of them trotting around us up a rise, lightly. You'd think they were playing in the snow. Maybe the big one is with them, but I lose them in the dark right away.

I hear Bengt and Tlingit and Henrick yelling and grunting behind me. I look back. They're jabbing and pounding at the last wolf on Ojeira, or trying to, but he's rolling away under the knives and the sticks. He wriggles out and runs away up the slope into the dark as if nothing happened to him. He stops with the big one and the others and they all look down at us. I think they do, but I don't know, because I can't more than half see them.

One rushes back in out of the dark, down the slope, straight toward Ojeira. He looks very big coming down at us. He isn't the biggest but I know he'll go through Ojeira like he's nothing. I'm so afraid my skin tightens and I step in his way and try to get my stick up but I get it snagged in his paws and it knocks away or I don't know how, but I drop it and he hits me and the weight of him coming at me that hard slams me back in the snow and he's on me, at my face. I try to grab his fur but he is right up at me and I can't get my stick, I have nothing.

I see Tlingit and his arm swinging like a windmill and I see Feeny's knife in his hand, and he punches it sideways and almost knocks him off me. But the wolf pushes back in at me and Tlingit punches him again and the wolf finally flinches and jumps off me to the side and falls into the snow.

He hunches and twists, but he doesn't get up, then he's still. I stare at him and my belly creeps. I should be glad he's dead, and I am, but my belly creeps all the same. I feel sick. It's from fear, probably, because the half-minute he was on me I thought this time I'd die. His fur's wet with blood I guess and there's wet in the snow now, and I look at him and feel sick still, more, churning. Probably fear, I suppose. I don't know.

I look up. The big wolf's looking down at us from the rise. The others with him look at us too. They don't rush in at us, they just stare. I stumble to my feet and look at him, and at Ojeira, who again, somehow, is alive still. He keeps gasping and breathing and looking at his middle where they were tearing at him. He starts almost laughing a sort of gut-hollow laugh and everybody is whooping.

"Yeah, you fuckers, fucking yeah!" Ojeira yells, which is surprising from the sight of him, because they did get him pretty well. But he's whooping, lying there, bleeding, facing it out to the wolves watching us. I'm wondering what it takes to kill Ojeira. He tries to get up, but flops back again, still laughing.

"Fuck you!" he yells, lying there.

I look up. The big one looks at me, it feels like, staring and staring, and then sudden as that he turns and goes into the dark. I can't see him at all. The others flow after him like smoke and they're gone. I stare, we all do, waiting, but we can't see anything or hear anything else of them. Bengt and Knox whoop and jump around like idiots again.

"Yeah! Fuck you, fuckers!" they yell again, and Henrick's smiling a sort of shocked and beaten half-happy. Tlingit too. Then I see Tlingit look to Ojeira, and his face drops. Ojeira's eyes are still open but he looks cloudy, not there, and I hear him trying to breathe, but he does not sound right. It's hard to tell by the fire but he looks like he's turned white or grey, or whatever you call the color when you're dead. But he's still breathing somehow. Even when he's dead he won't die.

I look at him, lift his jacket. The shreds of it, his sweater, everything's soaked in blood, and I see he's all ripped, they got into him. I don't know how they got so much of him. I know I broke my promise. We got them off, but we took too long. I tell myself we got one, but it doesn't help Ojeira. His legs are all ripped too, deep in the thigh. I thought we'd have more chance to save him. I look around the dark again, the dark on the snow, blood I guess. Our knives and sticks scattered everywhere, bloody now. Ojeira's out.

"He's going," I say.

The others stare at him. He's breathing, but less and less, a kind of shallow gravel noise.

Then I see the big one closer to us, on the other side of the slope, watching. The other wolves flank him, watching us too. The big one looks at me again. He leans low, like he's going to come in at us again, and I don't know if I'm ready yet but it won't be a choice, I'm sure.

I stare at him, waiting, breathing steam, and I haven't picked up any of the sticks or knives, like an idiot, but one is not too far from me. I dip down to get it in my hand without taking my eyes off him and we all stare like we did before, and the big one takes a step in at us, down the slope, very slow, pointing, and I think now he's going to really charge but he just looks at me, showing his teeth, pulling his nose back.

I have this brave theory that if we charged them we might scatter them, run them, get another one, even, but I am not as brave as my theory is, and I don't believe it as much as I would have to, to try it. I tense to go, once, but stop, my courage leaking and dumping out of me in buckets. I'm still stupid enough to say it.

"We could run at them," I say. "Scatter them maybe." The big one is up front. He looks like too much to run at. The others don't have anything in their hands, I don't think.

"We can wait with Ojeira, or go," I say. "Maybe they'll stay and watch him. Maybe he'll buy us a few minutes."

"For what?" Henrick says. I don't know. To think. I don't say anything. I don't want to tell them what to do.

"You sure he's going?" Tlingit says.

I nod.

"He's going before we get him anywhere," I say. "He isn't going home anymore."

We all stare at Ojeira. We don't try to find his wallet or say anything, we just look at him, and Bengt and Knox look at me, like hurt boys, again, then Henrick too, even Tlingit. Hurt boys, staring at me, and doing it anyway. Great are my ways.

We could leave without trying to get any more of the sticks or knives but I'm almost more afraid to do that than I am of trying to get them. I move as slowly and as lightly as I can, like a ghost drifting, to where the rest of my sticks fell behind me. I reach down, pick them up, watching the wolves. They react a little when they see the sticks. Or I think they do.

The others move too, as much as they dare, get sticks, knives, watching the wolves, like me. The sticks ahead of us we're going to leave there, rather than step toward the wolves. But I see my knife ahead of me, between me and the wolf, and I have to choose leaving it there or getting it. I edge toward it.

"Fucking leave it," Henrick says. I think he's right. But I look at the wolf, and edge a little more. He stares, and low-growls, and I stop. I start again, he growls a little louder, but I'm there, now. I reach for it and he snaps forward a little just as I snatch it up. I back up and stop, and he stops too. I wonder if I've offended him enough he's going to run on us.

I start back away, further. The big one advances on us. I stop again, and since I've lost my mind I lean in, a little, almost stepping in. I'm trying to say *'Don't come after us, we'll fight you.'* I back away more, then all of us back away and we only turn around to guess where we can put our feet in the dark. The rest of the time we're looking at Ojeira lying there as much as we're watching the wolves.

We keep backing away until we're far enough we can dare turn forward, and dare walking, leaving Ojeira there with them.

If I get any of the others out alive at least they won't have to damn themselves. I'm doing that for them. Seeing Lewenden off, letting Feeny go, Reznikoff, Ojeira. Somehow they're on my head. I look back at the wolves watching Ojeira like a curiosity, as if he's going to do something other than stop breathing. We keep going, waiting for the wolves to come at us. But more trees and dark are between us, and finally we're just slogging again, praying.

"Are they following us?" Henrick asks me.

"Yeah," I say, though I don't see them anymore.

7

WE MOVE A little faster without Ojeira. But we're more tired and more afraid than before, if that's possible. We're getting fewer, with regularity, and it seems like a clear road to none of us left at all. Sneaking away while they watch Ojeira die buys us a few steps, nothing more. I don't know what we bought them for, entirely. I don't have a sense anymore of where we're headed except what feels like away. West is a gone dream, if we could have ever walked to the coast, wherever it is. Maybe we'll see the sun a few minutes again, and find west again. But we keep going. All I want is to get a minute to think about what to do, but it's hard to think. I think about trying to make a deadfall. I've never done it but I know how it's done, and I know the ground is frozen too hard to dig, and I can't think of any other kind of traps we could make or what to make them with.

I stop, look back. I think of waiting for them, picking a place where we can wait and go at them, like madmen, but not as mad as walking along like stalking-goats. I don't know that they're going to follow in our steps anyway, they don't have to. They could be to our flanks or circling ahead, and waiting for us.

Something's gone out of me. Leaving Ojeira, or the last fight, or fear going through me, circulating like blood. Or the sight of the dead wolf on the snow that made me sick when I should have yelled like the others. I'm more frozen and stupid and beaten than before. But I get this idea of waiting for them, again. That's what I would do if I was trying to kill us. Get ahead, wait for us to walk along up, like the idiots we are.

I don't know what I have the courage to do anymore. By now we're good and haunted. They got another of us. We're into our fear with both legs, up to our middles, we're all praying to one thing or another, know it or not, like we have been since the plane started going down, and we're still praying, and wondering if it's working. Maybe we did all die on the plane, and we're walking in a dead dream. And the wolves are saying *'I'm your death, come to get you, I'm every wrong thing you've ever done. I'm the things you've killed, things you've left behind, come for pay.'* They aren't wolves at all. They're ghosts of all I've done, taking revenge. My head is dreaming in the cold.

The forest is less thick than it was, and clouds must have shifted or the cover is sparser, moon is coming down. I see openings here and there, not great clearings like the one we came from but little spaces, rocks bulging up, gullies that seem easier going than stepping over the roots and logs, we take those when we can.

We walk and walk. I slow down, even slower than the dead-leg crawl I've been doing, to try and catch a little breath. I try to think, again. I don't know if we're walking out of their turf or deeper into it. Maybe they could tell us which way is out, and let us leave, but they wouldn't tell us if they could. Because, I realize, they want us dead more than they want us out by now. We could go on forever changing directions and praying one of them will be the direction that isn't deeper into a place they're willing to protect by killing us.

"I think they might be circling ahead of us, like before," I say. Henrick nods, Tlingit and the others too. They stop, look ahead.

I stand there, trying to breathe, again, or think, again, at least think a little about where we're heading, so we aren't just circling back on ourselves or the wolves. The way ahead slopes down to a little lip. It looks like an easy slope to follow. I'm weak, so I follow what's easy. Tlingit follows my back, not even looking up. The rest take Henrick's line, I guess for the same reason. We've been tramping so long you just follow the back in front of you.

I get down as far as the lip, what I can see of it in the dark, and I start walking along it, easy snow. Then the air feels different, in the dark. It feels like there's nothing in front of me off the lip but air.

As soon as I realize I'm on a drop it drops away under me, the lip crumbles. I smack down on my hip and slide spinning, sticks flying, Tlingit tumbling after me. I'm banging my way down a face of ice and rock and dirt and roots are smacking me and one of my sticks falling after me shoots into my forehead and bounces off. I'm bang-sliding faster and faster, Tlingit too. I'm clambering to get my hand on anything that will slow me down and I'm dreading the launch when the cliff stops banging us and we're in thin air, before we land and die on whatever's on the bottom. We keep slithering, banging, faster and faster. I almost grab a root but it tears out of my hand, and then here it is, we're in air, empty, falling. I can't see anything. I'm waiting to fall a thousand feet and end.

Then we bang at the bottom. Rock or ice or snow, I don't know. I smack and bounce and roll, Tlingit does too. I realize we didn't drop far enough to die, or even break. We just dropped. I hear Henrick and the others yelling down to us. I realize they were yelling as we fell. I hear Tlingit groaning.

"Motherfuck," he says. "Jesus." Groans again.

"You break anything?" I ask him. "You okay?" I can barely see him, but I see him feeling his limbs and moving, to see if anything is fucked more than it was. He winces and grunts, but he says, "I'm okay."

I think I'm okay too. Everything hurts, my head's ringing, like I got hammer-punched, again, and the wounds I got from the wolves before are pulsing and pounding, and some new things hurt enough I think maybe I did break something, or several things. But I can move without crying.

I yell up to the others.

"We're okay," I yell. I try to see them up at the lip, and I think I make heads out, Henrick's and the others, but they could just be branches. I try to look along the direction we were heading, down here, wherever we are. I can barely see, but I can make out whatever this cliff is, it doesn't disappear soon.

"Keep heading the way you were," I yell up to them. Try to keep in sight of the ridge, if you can." I look ahead again.

"Okay" I hear Henrick yell.

"We'll try to meet up, if this bluff drops, ahead. Okay?" I yell.

"Okay," Henrick yells back. I still can't see them. But Henrick doesn't say anything else, and I guess they've gone.

"Fuck," Tlingit says.

"Yeah," I say. I realize that might be the last we see of Henrick, or Bengt and Knox. The terrain might push them away from the lip, they might lose it, or this face might run forever. We'll split wide and never find each other and either make it back or die in our separate ways.

I find myself praying they'll be alright, or that I will. I'm praying to the love of my son, my wife's love of my son. I think if the wolves are watching Henrick and the others they'll see they're fewer now, and maybe leave them alone. Maybe down where Tlingit and I have fallen, that break of land between us, could be some kind of boundary. Maybe we're away. But there's a little moon, and I look back, and I think I can see an easier slope behind us, I don't know how far, but it looks like a place wolves could come down easily if they wanted. I couldn't make it out before.

I wonder if Henrick and the others could get down that way. It looks too far back in the direction we last saw the wolves. I don't think they would have had it in them to backtrack that far. They're gone by now anyway. I hope again we'll find them ahead.

I feel my pocket. My knife is there. I'm glad it isn't sticking out of my side. I see some of the sticks we made scattered on the snow, they fell down with us. Tlingit and I pick them up. I look in front of us and I head away with Tlingit.

Imaginary advantages are keeping me going. But I realize that nothing we try, or fall off, is going to change anything. I look ahead, following the face of the bluff. Sure enough the terrain starts to split us away from it. I hope we'll still be able to get to someplace we could possibly ever find the others, but I don't know.

We let the slope force us down, and as we drop down another slope rises across from it, bounding us. We're in a gully stretching as far ahead as I can see. Nothing to do but follow it.

"This is some fucking thing, isn't it?" Tlingit says, lifting one boot after the other, like me.

I breathe out. It is.

"We going to live it out?" Tlingit asks. He doesn't want an answer. He's just saying it out loud. We go on a long time, boot after boot, I don't know how long. I'm dreaming wolf-dreams, about wolves who aren't wolves at all. The wolf in the heart.

"You think they're okay?" Tlingit asks.

"I don't know," I say. "I hope they are."

"You think they've seen them again by now?" Tlingit asks. I keep going, ear cocked for paws in the snow or yells far away, terror from Henrick or the others or barks or yips or anything. I know they're too far to hear. We keep going.

The gully starts to blunt. The slopes are lower, not so towering. I can't see the rise we came from, or the cliff, or anything but where we are. Up ahead I think I see it broadening to flat land again. I even imagine it's curving toward the side where the cliff was. I get a little hopeful we might find the others, if the two trails met as soon as this, instead of in three days' walk.

As soon as I think that I remember the wolves getting ahead of us like they did in the clearing, and if the drop has opened out to the rise above it, we're walking into somewhere they might be. Which is foolish to worry about, because they're wherever they want to be.

We keep going, watching the mouth of the gully. I look at where it opens out and I try to see how the ground lies ahead of us, trying to think whether we should find a place to wait for the others, or cut back for them, or keep going and hope we catch them.

I'm very busy thinking this when I realize I'm forgetting the wolves, like all I have to wonder about is the easiest way to walk home. And finally, sure enough, we have one, on the rise above us, following parallel, looking down at us. He's alone, which makes me worry, the others are either behind me where I can't see, about to rush me from behind, or ahead of us, off quietly killing all the others.

I'm not surprised, and almost relieved, to see him. I look to Tlingit to see if he sees him and Tlingit's seen him already, maybe before me, and he's watching him too. We both seem to think the thing to do is keep walking, for now.

Then we see another one, on the rise on the other side, above us like the other.

"What do we do?" Tlingit says. As if I know.

"Keep on," I say. I'm looking for a place where it looks good to try something, and I'm not seeing it yet, but I look ahead where the rises shallow out on both sides and I think if we're going to try anything, that's a place to do it without falling all over ourselves.

"Where it shallows out, you take that one, I'll take this one."

Tlingit thinks about that. I don't know what I'm thinking, I can't think any more.

"We run them off, or get them."

Tlingit stares at his wolf. I look up at mine. They're both staring down at us, setting low, like before. I recognize them. I'm still worried about the other wolves, and the other guys, and wondering if these two tracked us from behind or were ahead of us, hard to say. I can't see tracks. They're just here.

I feel as sure as I can be of anything they aren't going to let us by, for long. They are setting low, looking at us, still as stones, ready to fly at us. I fumble my knife out of my pocket, and hold it along my stick like before.

"We charge them. If they run around on us, just turn around and charge them again. We keep doing it until they jump up at us, then we fight them until they run." Tlingit keeps looking at me. It makes a mad sort of sense, a hopeless sort, and I am mortal crazy by now, but so is Tlingit.

"You ready?"

Tlingit doesn't say anything. I take a breath.

Then I start yelling and running up the rise at the wolf closest to me, raising my stick and Tlingit does the same with his, each after our own wolf. My wolf and the other actually look halfway surprised. They spring up, split away and loop behind us. We both turn on them and charge again, like madmen.

They watch us coming, but they still don't jump at us, they jump to the side, go behind us, circle us. But as we each keep turning on them and trying to look like we're brave enough to go at them they're backing towards each other down the slope and they each look back to see what the other is doing. They look uncertain for the first time.

But I remember they've been better at this than we've been, every time. Sure enough mine hops around to the uphill side, looking down at me, ready to jump at me from above and close enough to do it, and I don't like how that looks at all.

I roar and charge up at him with my stick again, and Tlingit goes at his at the same time, and my wolf gets sick of the game. He backs onto his haunches and barks and jumps at me. I see him coming and I manage to drop to my knee without falling down the slope and get the back of my spear jammed in the snow thinking I can land him on it. But I'm scared, I change my mind and come back up to drive it into him as he falls on me and he is stuck.

I'm holding him on the stick and holding his weight and mine from tipping over backwards down the hill, but he's barking and reaching at my face with his teeth, snapping, getting closer. I think he might be the one who got on my face before, back at the plane, and remembering his teeth on me I'm terrified, and as quick as that he gets my arm in his teeth and bites down and rips. I flinch back, turn his weight downhill and throw him down away from me to the snow, and then I fall after him, I hit hard. I get to my feet, sideways, and jump back stagger back away from him.

I look at him stuck with that thing, I stare at him like an idiot. I feel sick to have done it. I should be dancing, but I'm sick. Like I was before. He's trying to pull himself off, I didn't drive it in enough or he's just so frantic pushing his paws into the snow and wriggling backwards he's coming off it.

"*Fuck you*," I yell, because he's trying to get free, instead of dying. And because I don't want to feel guilty for killing him. But he's making it look like he's getting free, or he will be, and I panic and roar again and jump on him with my knife, and fall away backwards again, leaving the knife. I'm flinching and jumping at everything he does. I remember his teeth too well. I think he is the one who was on me before. He still fights, thrashing and trying to get up, but then he stops trying suddenly. His paws go out from under him. He lies in the snow, blinking, panting, making a gravelling sound.

And I'm still afraid of him and sick and afraid to have killed him and I've never felt like more of a coward in my life. I've done my share of killing things, after all. He's making me think of things I don't want to. No time to anyway. Or the fear or whatever I needed to dig out of my guts to let me run at him is making me sick, like I thought before. I run in at him to grab my knife and jump back. I'm still afraid he'll snap up at me. I leave the stick in him and grab up my others and run back up the gully toward Tlingit in the dark with a new stick ready, the rest under my arm like before, which makes running awkward. But I'm not brave enough to leave them.

I can see Tlingit's wolf still circling him and snarling. Tlingit's held his wolf like this all the time I was busy with mine. He looks ready to jump at Tlingit or run, darting looks behind him and forward at us. I look at him, but I look around too because I'm sure we can't be this lucky to have just these two.

I'm waiting for mine to get back up and come after me. Or for the rest of them to come. But this one looks mad enough to rip us apart by himself and I want to tell him we did not come here to bother him. But his answer would be to rip my lying throat away, so all I'm going to be allowed to do is kill him.

I get my stick ready and we charge at him. He's backed toward a crop of rocks. He can jump up over it or come at us. He flashes his teeth, comes up at Tlingit, and Tlingit steps aside and falls backward. I drop my sticks and swing the knife at his side as he flies past me, turning in the air toward Tlingit, but I don't think I get him.

He drops to the ground and bounces up. I don't think I touched him at all. He hops left and right of us and then he lopes away a few paces, and looks at us. And then he streaks away, into the dark. He didn't look particularly afraid of us doing it, he just went.

We stand there, looking into the dark, listening, waiting for him to come out at us from the side or the back. I look at the rocks stacked up above our heads, lining the gully wall, covered in snow, and they're all black shapes in the snow and all hiding wolves, as far as I know. But I don't hear paws, or panting, and he doesn't show himself, he just leaves us to worry about where he is. I look all around, Tlingit does too. We stand and watch a long time.

"Gone for now," Tlingit says. I'm watching the dark and the rocks, afraid to let any bit of guard down.

I look down, suddenly, at my arm, where my wolf bit it. I squeeze it hard as I can above where teeth went in, or whatever happened. It didn't seem as bad at first, but now it hurts more than the ones I got before. It feels deeper. Tlingit and I look at each other.

"Come on," I say.

We scramble to get sticks and knives in our hands, again, and we head back out the gully the way we were heading, but we tumble down into a deeper, narrower part of the gully nearer the rocks, which makes me nervous.

When I turn to look back and up behind us there he is, on a rock or jumping off a rock down at us. This time my knees just fold. I fall backwards, and Tlingit is turning to look up when it lands on him and gets the back of Tlingit's neck in his mouth, but not enough to hold on and Tlingit knows he's trying to so he twists and jumps, with all his might, and the wolf falls off him into the snow.

I'm on my feet by now, and charging in at him, and Tlingit's up too but I go down face first in the snow. I slipped off some root or something I couldn't see, I don't know, but the snow comes up and hits me in the face again. Tlingit almost falls over me and the wolf springs right up at him, mouth open, as Tlingit's catching himself.

He gets Tlingit's neck again but the side this time, and Tlingit is so fast again the wolf doesn't get a grip. Or Tlingit shoves him so hard he comes off. But the wolf angles his head and strains to get around under Tlingit's throat. I scramble up and he's stretching and working his teeth forward under Tlingit's chin as hard as Tlingit's trying to pull him off, but he isn't bothering with me.

I get my stick up again and I drive at him, yelling. It shoots through him, comes out the other side. Tlingit blinks, yanks his head back. It just misses Tlingit's cheek.

But he shoves the wolf off now. He falls back, as I feel all the weight of the wolf on my stick again and I drop him down to the snow, like I did the other. I want to jump back away this time too but I hold on, lean the stick into him, afraid to let go or let it up, this time. He stops moving. I'm still as sick as glad and don't know why. Don't want to.

Tlingit grabs him up from the snow, hoists him, roars, and throws him, heaves him as far as he can across the snow, still roaring. It isn't respecting dead foes, but I don't blame him. I don't feel like crowing, either.

Sometimes it happens you have to do a final thing like this. You have to do it. You have to choose, so you choose. I look at the wolf in the snow where Tlingit threw him, shrinking already in the dark, and my mind is running off again, up roads I don't want it to run.

Tlingit's gone quiet, staring at it too. Maybe he's embarrassed of the whooping, maybe his past is shaming him. You dance for a dead seal, but never a wolf, whatever it did. When you kill a wolf you carry him on your shoulders, you lay a feast for him, you say you're sorry, wrap him in sacred things, give him a burial. You don't dance unless you're dancing your regret. If your father's trying to kill you, and you kill him, are you rejoicing? Are you alive, anymore, even? Maybe you carry your dead with you, and never lay them down, and they take you to death with them, one day. Day by day, they carry you over with them.

I pull the stick out of Tlingit's wolf and get my knife, and we set off. I feel myself worrying about the others, and I start to trot, best I can through the snow, which lasts about a step. But I try to haul faster than before, and Tlingit huffs along with me. We're half-dead but we want to be away.

I see dead trees ahead that I didn't see before. I see the first wolf, still lying sad and black in the snow. I take the stick out of him, which sickens me too, then I feel like being sick is disrespectful to him. If I killed him, I should be man enough to not be sick about it. You should do what you do and have the decency not to quibble. But not everybody gets to do things and never bother about them. I wonder if what made me sick was sadness instead of fear, or something else. I remember other dead animals I don't want to think about.

I try to find the ground I thought I saw before, ahead where it looked like the gully met the rise. Tlingit and I head out past the dead trees, into thick forest again.

8

WE KEEP GOING, watching the trees ahead, looking to the sides and behind us, all we can. I'm listening, but I can't hear much more than our feet thudding the snow, and our breathing. We're in even thicker trees now, and we slow down. I'm expecting to find wolves or the others or an ambush. But aside from little puffs of wind still blowing through it nothing's moving.

There's less moon than we had out in the gully. As we go I see shadows in the corner of my eye, and every time I'm sure a wolf is walking alongside us in the dark it isn't there. I stop over and over for shadows and little sounds buried in the wind. But there's never anything. Not the others, or a wolf. Finally I do hear something, a low growl, and I stop. Tlingit does too.

"You hear it?" I say. Tlingit stays still, listens. It's a wolf talking, or wolves, or it's growling, shreds of sound coming and going as wind wanders this way or that, like the river I thought I heard before.

We're afraid to move. I am, anyway, I stay still and listen, and hear another shred, then nothing. The ground seems to be dropping away again in front of us. I edge forward and there's another lip of hard snow and a bank dropping down. Coming closer to it I hear Henrick, I think. Not a wolf.

We edge out to get over the lip, and I look down. There isn't much moon but I can tell this isn't like the other one. It's just a little drop if you aren't falling ass over end. We climb down toward the sound, to the side and back of us. We overshot and got up over them somehow, but we found them.

"*That you?*" Henrick yells out to us, through the dark.

"*Yeah,*" I yell back, and wonder what I would have said if I was a wolf. When we get down where we can see each other, Henrick's standing and the others are sitting on their haunches, frozen, terrified, like we are. They're still thinking we might be wolves, not quite believing we aren't until they've stared at us a little. They're relieved to see it's us, finally.

"Did you see any?" Henrick asks.

"Two." Tlingit says. "We got the better of them." He's quieter about it now.

Bengt looks at us, surprised. Knox and Henrick too. Nobody's whooping, this time. They're just surprised.

"What about you?" I say.

"Four of them were over there," Henrick says.

"They just stared at us. We didn't have the balls to charge them and they didn't come at us. They just went. After a while."

"Did you see the big one?" I ask. Henrick nods.

"Yeah."

I look around us. I'm trying to think what they got out of staring at Henrick and the others, why they didn't go at them, and if they're going to come at us now. We're all watching the dark, which is what Henrick and the others were doing when we got there. I don't blame them for not going at them when they saw them. Four of them, with the big one. I don't know if I would have done any different except run away or surrender.

They look at me. They're all exhausted, scraped-up, scarred, freezing, dying. Too far from home.

I stare, like them, try to think what to do next. Bengt's staring at his boots, going to sleep, or going away.

Something comes flying at him, jumps out of the dark and locks on to Bengt's shoulder, I can't see well at all. He screams, falling over, his hands flying up. Henrick and Knox stare, eyes wide, a half-second, I probably do too. But I run at him and I see Henrick getting his stick up, about to charge too when he's hit sideways, like I was before. It smacks him into a tree before I've gotten to Bengt.

Before I can do anything to help Bengt, the wolf lets Bengt go, jumps off him. I turn to the one on Henrick, who's still against the tree, flailing his knife with one hand, trying to push the wolf off with the other. Then it flips away, just like that. I look to Henrick, on the ground, he's spent.

We all scramble to get to Henrick. He's got new bleeding. I wonder if they did it on purpose, run in and wound us, let us bleed, I don't know. I run over to Bengt, as well as I can run. He's bleeding too, I can't tell how bad. But he's awake.

I can't see Knox anywhere but we're alone suddenly. I look for Knox, expecting the worst. But he's sitting against a tree. He looks alright. I think he sat through the thing too scared to do anything. Nobody blames him, because not one of us didn't want to do the same thing he did. And he lived through it, sitting there holding his knees, so good for him.

Bengt sits down in the snow, heavy as a corpse. He just thuds down, bleeding like hell I see now, his face and neck bleeding into the snow. I try to think of how to wrap him up. He shakes his head.

"Sweet God," he says. And he starts to sob, very tired fearful small sobs, coming out of him in the cold. I watch him from a few feet away, waiting for him to be ready for me to wrap him up with something, stop him bleeding.

But he just sags, and stops moving, and I see he's died. Henrick sees.

"*Bengt!*" Henrick yells, and he runs over to him. But he's gone. I stare at him disbelieving, or believing too easily. I go to him finally and I thump and bump on his chest, like that's going to do something, but I don't know anything about reviving people, just sending them off.

We don't know what did it, he just stopped, too much of this, too much of everything, God reached down and got him or somebody pressed a button somewhere and he stopped, a wire snapped, who knows, like when a car goes pfft, he went off into the air or fell into a crack in the earth, like all of us do. I stop thumping on him. We all stare at him. We feel the worse, somehow, after Bengt than the others. Maybe too many. Maybe we feel it's coming closer to us the fewer of us are left.

I look at him another half-minute probably, feeling sorry for myself more than him. But I feel sorry for him all the same. Finally I reach to see if there's a wallet and there isn't one, it's gone if he had one. Taking wallets home to families starts to feel like thinking I'm going to get pie in the sky when I die, or like the magic town with the magic blankets I'm never going to get to. I feel his other pockets, inside his coat, come out with a loose parole card and a condom in a wrapper. Who carries a condom and their parole card loose in a pocket? I realize most of us die in the middle of all our trivia and idiocy and things we're not proud of, the stupid shameful details of failures or hopes, all in embarrassing states of incompletion, forty bucks in your pocket, half-finished whining letters, great things you plan to do, overdue library books and unpaid bills and traffic tickets and people who haven't forgiven you and things you haven't forgiven yourself for but hope to one day. I feel my lids getting heavy on me, which is a strange thing, in all this. The cold maybe. Shock, shock of death. I'm weaving too, standing there over Bengt. I think I am. I'm not sure, or the air or the mountains or the world are sliding under me, back and forth. I don't know his first name, or where he was from.

I feel something suddenly, and look down at my arm where the wolf in the gully got it, or I tore it on a branch falling, or both. I'm bleeding, from a little thing like this, quite a bit. My hand's crusted in blood, but new blood is coming down, sheeting over, dripping off my fingers, now. I hadn't noticed, and trying to remember I don't know what it was more, as bad as the bite was now I remember something tearing my arm as I slid down the drop. I did more of it falling off that ledge, maybe. I blink, slowly, thinking a cut from some branch I fell on is going to kill me and not the wolves. Luck of the draw.

I decide to stop thinking about who I can't get home, who I've failed and left out here, and I decide just to think I'm alive, for now, a few more minutes, hours maybe, whatever I get I'll take. I feel less greedy suddenly. I knew my son, I knew my wife. The wolves in the dream didn't take me from them before I knew them. Some dreams you wake up from and all is well, none of it befell you, the world is whole. I breathe cold in, cold out. I am grateful.

But things are drifting, I know, to an end not victorious. And I am drifting with them.

9

WE KEEP ON through the snow and the dark, fewer again. I stare at my boots, like I did when I had a wire tied on one of them. I remember on hunts in the snow with my father, watching his boots as we tramped in the snow, him telling me to walk in the holes his boots made so I wouldn't get stuck. I remember trailing and trailing those boots through the snow, and night, sometimes, hunts longer than they should have been, I suppose. But he didn't know when to leave off and never did. I keep going, listening for Henrick and Tlingit and Knox behind me, keeping them with me, or I think, anyway.

When I was a boy about the age my boy is now, I guess, my father came home from a hunt one night or some other thing full of whiskey or something, and something blacker in his eyes than I'd ever seen. As I remember, anyway. He had his pistol and he raised it, weaving gently, at my mother, who was at the stove, while I stared at him.

He said to her: "You piss me off," and as she turned around he shot her, in the chest. When I stood up with my mouth open he looked at me and put two in my chest. I never knew why I deserved the two. Maybe he just liked the rhythm, once he started.

I believe, though it might have been a dream, that from the floor where I fell what I saw happen then was he sat down on the bottom stair and put the pistol to his head and yelled his lungs out over and over like somebody crying. But I never heard a shot, because he didn't fire, if he ever even raised the gun to his head, or yelled out like that. Maybe I just wanted him to, and dreamed it while I lay there bleeding.

There were sheriffs and police at the hospital who came to see me and they said my father told them two men came in and took his gun and shot my mother and me, for thirty dollars in the flour-tin and my father's gun and a box of my father's bullets, and he got home after and found us. They asked me if that's what happened.

I sat in the bed for a long time getting words, but I never told them anything different from what he said. That's a hard thing to understand. I don't know why I did that for him. I might have done it for me. But they went away, happy enough.

They let him in to see me then. He stood at the end of the bed. "I guess bullets go right through you, too," he said. He looked nervous, as if he didn't believe what he just got away with, and was waiting for something else. "They said I was a hero, to get you here when I did."

Later he said he was sorry. He said something got in his brain and took him over, so it wasn't him that did it. I didn't believe that, but I didn't tell him I didn't. You live in houses that are damned, sometimes, and you stay, and when you leave you realize you're the house that's damned, so leaving didn't matter, anyway.

"You're a tough little animal," the doctors said, for taking those bullets and living they meant, though taking the bullets was nothing. After my holes healed up I went home from the hospital and the house was emptier, as you'd expect it to be. I wanted to run away and didn't. In stories they say ghosts stay where there's unfinished business, but I can't think of any business that ever is finished, for anybody, ever. I went back to school a little, long as that lasted, and I went on hunts with him. I planned to kill him every day, for a while, but that was a dead-born plan. It turned out I am not that kind of killer. Some other kind, but not that kind.

I think I started my habit then of never going to sleep. I sleep, but I don't lay me down and pray the Lord and go there willing. I stay awake until it comes over like somebody clubbing you from behind, because I can't go on awake anymore. My body does it I guess, but not me. If I can choose, I'm awake.

He would come to the door of my room in the middle of the night, I don't know why. To see if I'd run off, or if I was loading his rifle in the dark, to kill him, with a flashlight under my covers where other boys read books.

"You're a night animal," he'd say. "A little wolf." He told me a wolf was an unhappy animal, happier dead, like any unhappy animal.

I was left to reason he was helping me when he shot my mother and me. Even if it wasn't him who did it. Even if he was a hero for taking me to the hospital. He'd tell the story, forgetting it was him who shot me, and feel very grand. I didn't remember often seeing him proud and he was proud of that, throwing his son in a car and riding him to the emergency room after dropping him like an elk. It was a lie he believed, like others.

"You're very lucky," the doctors told him, "Thank God you got here when you did," they said. And he nodded and said "God bless you, doctor. Thank you for saving my boy."

You live in a damned house, lies buzz the air like flies. You wave them aside, try to ignore them, you go from wake to sleep when you have to and go on. When I was much littler I had asked and asked my mother for a brother and a sister. "I'll be your sister, when you want me to be, and you be your own brother," she said. It was a given, I guess, my father wasn't going to be anything but what he was. But I was glad, after, sitting in the hospital bed, nurses looking at me sorry and round-eyed, and home, after that, that she never gave me any brothers or sisters. I was glad I was alone so no one would have to bear it but me.

I feel like I'm dreaming, while I step over this branch, that root, winding my way. I have to think to know if I'm awake or asleep, blood leaking, what blood's in me slowing and freezing, no food, no sleep in me or next to none for years. I'm still afraid in a half-dead way. I remember what the wolves felt like on me, what they might feel like on me again, how it might go another time, if they get further with me than they did. I keep looking to the others, listening for them, counting in case we've lost somebody else. In case somebody's fallen away silently like Bengt and in my blur I haven't seen.

The trees are much thicker again. It's harder to spot the others now. Much as we're sticking to each other, we're having to weave through a thicket in this trench. But we seem to have everybody that's left of us. We keep looking back up at rises and ridges out to the blind sides of us. Here's to us who was like us, devil the few and all dead anyway, my father said, and totted his tot, cleaned his wounds, whatever they were, from the inside, from his glass.

You walk in a night forest, death along with you for the walk, you remember things, dream things, get lost, step after step. Even this cold, this fearful, your mind wanders. You've lost a mile not knowing you were walking. I catch myself sniffing the air to see if I can smell water or wolves anywhere. I hear our boots thump and our breathing but I try to block it as if I'm going to hear a wolf walking in the snow, which I won't, or a howl or a yelp, which I won't. After they get another of us they'd howl again maybe, but not yet.

I listen anyway and I think I hear breathing or rattling or a raven far off. I'd like a raven for company for us, or an elk, or a caribou, but there's been nothing. No birds, no foxes, nothing on the hoof, just us and the wolves. I wonder if it's a dream, like I thought before, if I did die in the crash and I'm bleeding on the snow by the plane while the wind covers snow over me forever, and I'm just walking now, a ghost though snow forever, paying for something.

I lost a long time ago any idea of what west might have been, if west was ever the way to go. I start dreaming again about a magical river that will lead us to the coast. To a magic town with people who'll take us and give us magic blankets as warm as love and that stop the wolves from eating us.

I stop to listen to the hissing raven sound, and again I think it could be water. It's my magic river, I think. I dreamed it into being and it's going to lead us home. There isn't enough wind in me to laugh.

But I look at the others, and try to focus my eyes on them, and I listen.

"I hear water. A river maybe," I say.

They nod, but it doesn't mean anything to them.

"We find a river, it might lead to the coast. A village somewhere," I say.

I wait for them. Henrick nods.

We start to cut toward the sound. We have to, because I see the ground rising up so steep now to our side. The sound is getting louder, funneling through this thicket, I guess, from wherever it is. But it can't be far. It's water.

We make for it and like everything else in this place it seems like we're slogging and standing still at the same time. But the ground starts to drop further and open up, I think. Or I'm making things up in the dark. But the sound is getting louder too. Thinner though. It sounds less like a river the closer we get to it.

It's been bleeding light into the sky little by little and I finally realize daylight is coming, such as it's going to be. Then it seems it's gotten as light as it's going to get today, just a pale ghost of day, for ghosts. This might be the last day. Or there's another, and there's going to be a few minutes of it depending on when you call it gone. A day of dawn then night, or dusk then night.

As long as I've lived with it, it feels like something that should happen on some other world. But I'm glad for the light we get. I tell myself that the little curl the sun is going to do on one edge of the horizon must be south, so west must be to our flank. Unless with the blood going out of my head, the sun rises and sets in the north, instead of south, but I think it's south. I've known my whole life, but now I'm tired, and bleeding and don't know what I know, the days of the week or my mother's name. I try to remember my son's name, and I do. Then my wife's, I remember hers too. Mine's gone for the minute. I know it but it isn't here just now, I couldn't say it but it will come back. I don't think I'll lose my name yet. It'll come.

We keep going, following the sound. I start to feel colder air coming off the water. I hear it running now. We start dropping down toward it and now I feel like we're on top of it and then we get up a little rise and the bit of daylight catches ice or water and I see it's a decent stream, or a good little river, half frozen but I'm blessing this river and looking at it like holy water. We feel a little better but thinking a river will lead us to the coast after walking for two weeks isn't going to save us. But it feels better to hope we have something to follow.

But the smell of water and the bit of morning light has me giddy and we dare to drop down in the freezing sting of water running over the ice at the edge and drink. Cold as we are I haven't thought about being thirsty but we're all frozen, dry as dead men. We're cupping it up in our hands but that hurts our hands too much so we just stick our faces in, that hurts too but we do it, looking up as we're drinking, all around, in case something's coming at us while we have our faces stuck in the water. I realize we're a pack of animals, like they think we are.

I sit back and look, watch water dripping down me and I don't even care that getting this wet with freezing water will probably kill me. I sit there looking out and seeing if that was enough water for me. I realize I'm using the water for food, trying to fill out my belly. But I've had enough I guess, the others have stopped too by now.

Water in us, we're up again, looking right and left and behind us. I'm trying to scout the way ahead best as I can for how we're going to make a way if we're following this thing but also for where they might come at us from, if they do. Each time they leave us alone a little I wonder if they're done with us, if they think we've learned our lesson, gotten the idea. But no, apparently we're still getting it wrong. We're not going the way they want us to go. Or like I said they just don't like us, and won't like us till we're dead. Then they may like us fine.

Whatever way the river's running I figure is to one coast or other, coast, north or west. I can't figure anything from the sun anymore. But I feel like the river is going to lead us to the west, I don't care, as long as it leads us somewhere.

So we follow it, we have a course, and we forget the obvious that the wolves don't care that we know where we're going now, or imagine we do. They still hate us for being where we don't belong and more than any wolves in the history of wolves, they are not going to put up with it.

We keep along the river down around a wide bend that feels like it's going in a big loop to nowhere at all, the curve's so big, but we follow it, and it occurs to me there are places we might cross, if we're brave enough, that would put the river between them and us. I like that idea. They're smart enough to stay out of the river and not drown. A wolf won't go into a river after an elk or a caribou unless he's starving mad, he'll just stand on the bank and wait for it to come back out, if it can't get across, and he'll kill it then, when it's climbing back out, slower and weaker.

I've heard of them forgetting all that if they're after other wolves or something else they feel they have to kill something that's a matter of necessity to them to get done. They'll chase wolves they don't like into a river and as good as drown trying to kill them, the same with something coming after their young, a bear, whatever it is, anything too close to their den. But I still like the idea of being on the far side of this. I'm wishing we'd come on a place to cross sooner, but everywhere I've looked at has looked like a good place to drown in, in the state we're in.

We come down the long curve. I'm looking at a sharper bend where there are rocks it looks like we might hold on to and not get washed away, if we don't get ourselves smashed on them. I know it can't be too deep, but it doesn't have to be that deep to get over your head and washed downstream and die. I wouldn't mind, almost. That seems like a relief maybe too. But no.

"You think you could get across there?" I ask the others. They look at it. They all know the other side would be a better place than here, but it still looks like the river could kill us so we're not in a hurry to climb into it. The more we look at it the harder it looks to cross. I start to think maybe we'll keep on downstream, hope for better.

"Maybe we could find better," Henrick says. I nod.

"Maybe." There must be a place that looks less like it could kill us. But we're close to the edge, or where the ice starts, anyway, looking like we might want to cross.

I see something moving. I look up, so do the others. It's the wolves. They're trotting, the big one and the others, edging along watching us. They're running right to left in front of us, keeping a distance but angling closer, then closer still, running up and down along the bank watching us.

We back toward the river. I'm damned if it doesn't look like the big wolf doesn't want us to leave. He'd rather keep us out of the river and kill us to be sure we'll never come back. But I know we'll have some chance in the water.

"Fuck it," Henrick says, and steps off the ice into the water, and starts across, Tlingit and Knox splash in after him. I don't know if the wash will kill us, but we're going. I watch the wolves, and wait to go last. I want there to be a chance they won't bother to come in after us, they'll wait us out, or watch us cross and finally give up. Something has to be a boundary for them, if it wasn't the clearing or the cliff I fell off or the woods beyond that, maybe the river. But no.

The big one is coming at us, running down the bank, he doesn't want us in the water, he's going to hit us before we get too far and get away from him. The others charge with him. I'm not in the water more than a few seconds before they're jumping right off the bank after us. I stumble and splash backward through the water hoping it's going to get deep enough to lose them. I look at

Henrick and I can see he's having it hard to cross but he's doing it. I keep backing up, holding my stick, watching the wolves.

"Don't step in a hole," I call to Henrick. "You go under you'll be gone. Okay?"

Henrick nods, still feeling his way across, using the rocks, Tlingit after him, fast as he can. Then Knox. After a few more steps Henrick loses the stick he has, or lets it go, because it's too hard to hold the rocks and a stick at the same time.

It's stronger than it looks, the wash, and everybody has to hold hard. I have to use all I have to hold my footing and not go down. I'm cutting my hands grabbing the rocks and I'm trying to keep my balance and keep my stick out ready. The wolves are splashing right behind us, coming up on me. The pain in my legs and my middle from the cold feels as sharp as anything the wolves got into me before and it seems to be mounting, getting worse as I go, and we're all panting and feeling our insides trying to crawl up into our chests, trying to stay ahead of them.

I stumble backward all the faster and take a big fool step and drop in deep, and lose my stick. But thank God, the big wolf is over his head already. He's barely holding on, half-swimming. I see the cuts in him with his fur wet. He bobs up and down, still coming at me, and suddenly he slips and the water gets under him hard and he's washed loose.

He bangs into the smaller wolf downstream and knocks him into the current too and the third looks to the big wolf washing down, unsure, suddenly. And he loses his footing too and all three are suddenly washing down toward a wash hole, back toward the bank we came from. They get their paws under them and start to climb back out and slip but they get out to the ice. They look smaller, spike-furred, and I see cuts and gashes on the others too

I didn't know were there, I don't know when they got them from us but somewhere they did. They stand on the ice, watching us. I look ahead to Henrick and the others and they are still okay. They're getting across, step by step, and we're happy the wolves got washed back away from us. We're almost laughing.

But Knox does something, he's distracted seeing them wash down and he's so happy to see it he loses his feet, slips off a rock, I don't know. He goes under suddenly but he pops back up grabbing for rock. He gets hold and looks okay again but before he's steadied himself he slips again, into the same hole or something. He goes under again, and this time he comes up a few feet downstream but he's washing on to more rocks I think he'll get a hold of, and he just doesn't.

He doesn't even look worried. He just sort of touches the rock and slides around it like he doesn't understand he needs to grab it.

"Grab that!" I yell to him but he's past it, and there is another he's coming up on and I point to that.

"Grab that one! Knox!" By now Henrick and Tlingit have seen and they're watching him and yelling too, and I'm starting downstream for him but he's already far. Somehow Knox can't get a hold on the next rock either and he dips and slides over a ledge and drops under and when he comes up he's going faster. I watch, and so do the wolves, as the current shoots him straight for the bank where the wolves are.

He goes under again and comes up again trying to push and swim away from the bank but he's getting sucked across into the far shallows and he manages to get to his feet a few yards from the wolves.

"Get back in the water. Get to the middle!" I yell, and the others are yelling his name, and the wolves run and jump off the bank into the shallows before he can get himself back into deep enough water fast enough. They circle behind him and the big one pulls him down with his teeth and the others swarm over him.

We stand there barely holding on, helpless again. One of the wolves pulls Knox up on the ice by the bank, red dragging over it, and they rip into him again and then stop. They circle and trot around him and then stop again, mouths red, soaking wet, looking across at us.

"Go. Keep going across," I yell to Henrick, and he turns and pushes the rest of the way over, working every step, looking back. I look back at Knox too, on the ice, and the wolves watching us. I watch to see if they come into the water after us again. They don't. They just watch us.

When I think my legs aren't going to work anymore I see Henrick get to the ice on the other side, and flub around all eager trying to get up over it but it keeps breaking under him and dropping him back in.

Finally he sees the ice is broken closer to the banks further down. He makes for that. He gets his knees up on rocks, and stumbles forward back on to thicker ice, and then snow and he's home. Tlingit does what he did and I come out behind them.

When I get on to the snow I look across again as the wolves look at us and trot away, along the bank and then up over a hump of snow and disappear. They left Knox there on the bank, but I'm relieved there's snow piled blocking where he is from here, so I can't see him anymore.

We're jumping up and down and half-crying with the pain of the wet freezing cold. Now we're out in the air, the air feels weird warm, if it's possible, over the bone pain. But whatever that cold did to our flesh we are paying for now, there's a long deep pain coming out and I wonder if the water's killed the last of us.

Henrick's kneeled down then gone over on his side and he's lying in the snow balled up. Tlingit stays jumping and stomping, I jump and stomp too and hope the pain is going to stop before my heart does. Henrick looks bad, I think it did something to him, his insides are gripping, or something. I go look down at him.

"You've got to get up," I tell him. He nods, understands, I think. He should be up and moving or something worse might be happening to him. I realize though we need a fire right now, and that I didn't think of that, didn't pick the spot for its firewood. I didn't pick it at all.

"Let's make a fire," I say, and I hustle toward the trees. It hurts like hell to move but I tell myself it's good to move, so I keep going. I think if we get a fire going we'll stay alive. But it feels like if it isn't going in about a minute we'll die. I scramble for whatever pieces I can and Henrick and Tlingit have hustled over with me to do the same and we lay it down a little off from the river because cold air is rushing over the river from the water, a little in from the bank it feels warmer.

We don't want to use the pieces we've carried for clubs. None of us feels like we won't need them again, and they got soaked anyway crossing, like our sticks did, and we've lost those, anyway.

I fumble for the lighter in my top pocket. I'm glad I had it there, because I was so scared stupid I didn't do anything to keep it dry crossing, and the water was just about as high as the pocket it was in, and was only higher when I stumbled, but it's dry enough to spark and it lights.

The first twigs won't light at all but I keep the flame on drying them and heating them until they will but I see the little bit of fluid through the casing and there isn't much, so I wonder if they'll catch before it runs out, and then it hisses and sputters out. I flick and flick it and it sparks and hisses but doesn't light again, and my heart is getting tighter and tighter, and our clothes are stiffening on us, turning to ice.

I see there are needles on one twig that have dried a little, next to the ones that burned away when I had the thing lit. They're yellowed brown and look dry enough to catch, so I spark the wheel at them and I can see sparks hitting and glowing and needles curling away but not lighting.

I try the other lighters Tlingit got from Feeny but they got too wet, they're no good, not even sparking. I think they might dry eventually but we need heat now or that's that, got past the wolves and froze dead on the spot. I shake the first lighter and hold it upside down a minute and try again and it lights and blows out before the needles or the twig light, so I go back to just trying to get sparks on the needles.

The guys have made a wall around it to stop the wind. We're shivering, wet, dying by inches maybe, and we're watching this stupid disposable flint-wheel sparking pointlessly, over and over.

The needles still don't light, and then suddenly one glows and curls and catches, and the needles next to it that have dried out catch, and the tiny bit of sparrow-leg branch it's on catches, and I hold another twig up over it and get a little flame going. I burn my fingers but I'm not dropping it if it burns my whole hand off. I lower it to the other twigs and hold it there, my fingers probably burning off by now and I don't care, I can't tell the difference between that and the cold anyway, and some bigger pieces catch and I let go and we lay on. We all hover over it to be warm but also out of fear it will blow out, there are gusts that could blow it out it seems.

"What do we do, take our clothes off so they dry?" Henrick asks. Sitting out here naked in the wind doesn't seem too happy, either.

"I don't know," I say. "We get it going big enough we'll dry a little, maybe." Henrick nods.

"Let's get more," he says, and he huffs back to the trees, Tlingit with him. I stay here to guard the thing, or stay warm, probably that. They hustle back with some broken pieces of green branch they twisted off, more like boughs, needles and all, but even green needles like that are good, they go up like crazy for the little time they burn and help dry the wood. Doesn't last long, but doesn't hurt.

We all take turns running for more and we get it going to a ridiculous size. We can't get warm, however big it is, but we don't feel as bad as we did.

"We should eat something," I say, because I realize with nothing inside us we might all sit down for naps now and just freeze like meat in a freezer.

We pull what wet crap we have from our packs. Bags of chips and peanuts, a couple of granola bars. Tlingit's got an apple, somehow, and I'm amazed he's been carrying this red round thing around that survived a crash and getting chased by wolves, it's been riding in his backpack like school lunch on a field trip. He tries to bite into it and I see from his face it's frozen, but he chews it and passes it to Henrick and we all get a bite each and we think we're in heaven. With most of us dead, we still can chew a frozen apple and think we'll live.

We eat some peanuts but we have to choose between starving later or dying of cold now and I don't know how frozen apple is on that account. Or how much food will stop us from freezing to death. But we guess a few bites each might keep us alive.

I look back across the river, for the wolves, and I still can't see them anywhere, and I wonder if they really can't get across, if this was all we had to do, get across a river, to live. We feel a little better, on this side, and we have our river to follow, and we're half-warm for now or less frozen, and half-dry, or less cold-soaked, and we start to think maybe the others who died were the ones to die and we're the ones who lived through it.

Maybe we're looking back, imagining looking back, telling the story of how guys all around us got killed but we came through, like my dad in the bar, because we've lived through everything so far, so that must mean we'll live through this. Ojeira and the rest thought the same thing, until they stopped breathing. But we're happy we're on one side and the wolves are on the other, and that the wolves tried but couldn't make it over. We're happy that if we're bright enough to follow the river and not die of something else, we might get to the ocean.

Finally I tell myself we're dry enough, which we aren't, at all, or as dry as we'll get, but as hard as it is to leave the fire I feel like we should go.

"Should we move?" Henrick asks. I nod, and we pick up our packs and our knives and head on. We're excited we might be through, and we want to rush away, rush out of it, if we can. But we all look back at the fire like we're leaving home.

We get back on the slog downriver. We keep going, sloping down sometimes, over long flats others, but we keep going, and the light seems to be holding, still, and no wolves for what seems a very long time now. You want to think things. Hopeful things.

We follow another long curve, another big looping patient bend we have no patience for, but we keep going, and there it is, a round little lake, looking at us, not that big even, a stupid little frozen pond, and suddenly I don't see my river or what I thought was my river coming out of it. It dead-ends.

We sag, looking at it, but we keep along the curve of the lake, better than halfway around, most of it ice, until we've seen all sides, and the stupid stream we thought was a river dead-ending in it, the river we thought was between us and the wolves isn't anymore.

"That's done," I say.

I sit in the snow. Look at it. Light is suddenly going paler, pale grey, way home is gone. My hand is red-black again, new blood, the old washed off in the river. The sky looks like a giant eye, closing.

10

WE COULD KEEP going but the river's discouraged us. Maybe they've forgotten us or don't know there isn't a river between us anymore, and we're going to stumble mad with cold to our deaths without even knowing we've gotten away. I feel sure I have less than the required amount of blood in my brain. I'm blinking and frozen down to some place between slow-wit and half-wit and numb. Maybe we'll give up here and let them have us, when they get around to understanding we're still here. When they trot around the end of this fucking fool pond, no more river for us to laugh at them across, and stare at us, deciding who to choose next. It doesn't look like a bad place to quit. When you think of all the times in your life you might have, I wonder if the one you end up giving into is just that, the one you end up giving into.

"What do we do now?" Henrick says. I'm silent, because I want to say '*Light a fire, and lie down and die.*'

"Keep going," I say finally.

But none of us moves. We all sit, more ready to die probably than we were yesterday or this morning, whatever morning was. We sit watching the water, the far curve of it, to see if wolves are there yet. If they've come down to meet us. Knowing, unlike us, where the river ended.

Finally I take off my jacket and pull up my sleeve to look at my arm. It isn't very good. I wipe some snow on it, and it doesn't look much better. I see the bites, but I was right, there's a tear, maybe the wolf did it but from how it feels and remembering how it felt it was the damn branch, my fool fall. My life of fool falls. I wonder what God thinks of me and my performance so far. Nothing, probably. Henrick and Tlingit look at the tear in my arm, assessing, I know, like I'm assessing. They're guessing if it will kill me too. It's still oozing blood, not stopping. I don't know why. Maybe too deep.

"That'll be okay," Henrick says, which is nice of him, but he's not stupid. It doesn't look like it's going to help me get out of here, that's clear enough. I use my knife to cut a strip off the shirt I found on the plane and tie the strip around my arm as tight as I can, and hope for the best.

There's a calculation to make, like everything, but I don't bother to make it because I know it isn't good, but what of it, and the wolves will probably find us again and kill us. Who gives a fuck any more. I get my jacket back on fast as I can, half-wet or not. My name's come back to me, like the name of somebody you knew once, I have it again, but I feel I may not have it long. I forget myself, down to meat and bones and thinking that I'll keep going.

We get up, start walking, leave the pond or the lake and the dead-end river behind us. I don't come up with any more great-general ideas. At some point, there got to be less fight in me than what's required. Or seeing Knox or Bengt added to Ojeira added to the others finally took it away from me.

So if there's a plan, it's blunder along, pray we don't get taken from the earth by all the things that are stronger than we are.

Even doing that is as good as giving up, because more than likely, they will find us again, keep coming for us, and take the last of us and be done with us.

It's still daylight, though I thought it was going. I've lost track of when there isn't going to be any more of it, and it's barely light at that anyway, it's like weak water. Half-day. We're all marching, half-stumbling, bloodied, battle-scarred, pale, starving, through another clearing, one of a chain of clearings strung together ahead of us, broken by little clumps of trees.

"I should have stayed home," Henrick says. "Worked at liquor-store. I'd be with my daughter right now."

I don't know if he's talking to me or mumbling to himself. I shrug.

"Or dead in a hold-up," I say. He looks at me, doesn't appreciate the perspective. I'm apologetic but I'm too tired to apologize.

"At least she's known you," I find myself saying.

Henrick keeps walking, not much comforted.

"She won't remember me, though." That he's realized this seems to be the saddest thing in all the world he could ever think of. That all he's known of his little girl so far will never have happened. He'll be dead, and what he thought his life was will be taken away from what he thought the world was. I don't know if she'll remember him or not, or if it will matter to her. Maybe better she doesn't.

"Maybe she will," I say, finally. He shrugs, keeps going.

"I want mine to remember me," Tlingit says. "He better."

I nod. We fall quiet again, marching. My legs feel like part of the snow. All of me does, even my thoughts, what's left.

"I want to go home," Henrick says, after a while, like he said before. I know he does. Tlingit and I don't say anything.

The little clearing runs into trees again, and then we come out into the next clearing, a bigger one, a great white sea of snow like the one we crashed in.

In the distance on the snow, I see black shapes dotted across. For a minute I think we're back in the clearing where we crashed, seeing dead bodies. I feel panic, that we've come in a big circle back to the plane and the dead. But then I stop, we all do, and stare at the dots. They look like wolves, and I feel another panic.

"Is that them?" Tlingit says, squinting.

But none of them is moving. They're just lying in the snow.

We keep on, staying on the edge, in the cover of the trees, and watch the wolves, or whatever we're looking at. Maybe they're rocks or clumps of twisted wood, or dead caribou, we're hoping. But we keep edging along, watching them, and finally when we get close enough I see they are wolves. They're dead, dried and frozen.

We stop, staring at them. As long dead as they look we're afraid they're going to get up and start running at us, we're just as afraid of dead wolves as live ones. They're bits of tattered hide hanging off cold bones, haunting us from there.

We're still cringing behind the trees, hiding from them when we know they're dead. They aren't our wolves, anyway, they've been there too long. We finally cut across the clearing, go look at them.

"It's another pack," I say.

Henrick and Tlingit nod. We stare at the carcasses, and see ourselves, lying there, another bunch of dumb animals who went to somewhere they shouldn't have. I look around, farther across the clearing.

There are other carcasses too, some caribou, antlers sticking up out of the snow, meat stripped, part-bone, part dried-out hide.

It feels like a dead place. There's more wind or a front is coming or I'm getting even weaker but it feels colder, much colder, bitter down to more bitter.

I keep staring at the dead wolves. All they fought and hunted and played and mated, lying there. They don't look like animals to me anymore. Just meat and hide in the shape of what was.

If these dead ones were hunted down by the pack hunting us, I'm sorry for them. Anything dead I feel sorry for now. I wonder if they were afraid, like us. I wonder if they knew they were dying.

One of them is lying half on his side, away from the others, his head turned back, face half in the snow, and my mind is wandering, again. This far away, walking into death, and my mind's running places where it isn't wanted. You go through your time, you'll gather places you never want to go to again, but your head will go there without asking. To gall you, I guess. Or I don't know why.

11

THE LAST HUNT I went on with my father was cold. Almost as cold as this. He had a pint bottle he would pass to me, then curse me to get it back to him sooner. I remember pouring a sip into the snow for every sip for me when he wasn't looking to mess his day up, leave him short for the way back.

"You piss me off," he said, waiting for the bottle. He might not have said that, might have been something else, but that's what I heard. It was what he said to my mother when he shot her. It rang in my ears, along with the bangs of the shots. As you'd expect.

He said he wanted into the woods that day. He said he was after a wolf he was convinced was there. He'd been after him all his life, feuding with it. He'd tracked it, shot at it, tried to trap it, turned around and seen it watching him, tracking him while he thought he tracked it. I don't think there was ever a wolf. Or it wasn't the same one, just different ones he'd met or imagined. The wolf in the woods was his sanity, what remained, or his madness, a thing he made up to wander the woods while he slept, like a dream blowing across all he was insensible to, watching for him.

It was air, a thing he said. There never was any wolf. It was a joke, and meant something else, or it was a story of his father's, or a legend he liked to pretend for himself, but he lost the difference. It was the murder of my mother he made into an animal that didn't exist, that he had to hunt down, that he had to die finding or die with, that he could blame, or put his mind's hand on, that he could make into something less awful than it was.

But it stayed a fearful thing. It was his ally and his enemy, his protector and undoing. He was full of blood to go looking for it. It hunted him when he wasn't hunting it, and he feared it when he wasn't laughing at it, or thinking he could get it. Maybe he invented it just for that. To think it was something he could kill and put an end to, because that was a solution he understood. But that escaped him, too.

Why he thought he was going to find him that day I don't know. But he was full of going-to-get-him-today. He sounded final. He knew he was going to get something that day.

There were black-tailed deer, which is what we were really out after, dinners, under his jokes and raving. He skittered up one wall and down another. When he wasn't made of iron and cold and anger and regret, when he forgot himself and had enough to drink, he floated off and raved. He raged, he roiled in what he did to my mother, without ever mentioning it. No, it was only the wolf in the woods that he saw in his sleep.

We plodded through the snow and passed his bottle and I saw one. A black-tail. Not huge, a good size though, down a slope, trotting to the left, after I don't know what, then stopping, trotting the other way, to the river that was there, to drink.

"Well, there's some dinners," he said. He went to take his gun up, and stopped.

"You want it?" he said.

I shrugged. No I didn't. He shrugged too, like I made no sense to him.

Then he looked suspicious, because that's what you are over anything that doesn't make sense. It's how he looked standing at the bottom of my bed in the hospital when I was little, with the hole in me he'd put there. But he took his rifle up the rest of the way. He didn't take much time sighting, he just raised the gun and fired. The deer dropped without much fight and my father was already walking, then trotting down the slope. Excited, I guess, to see his work.

I trailed him down, watching his back go down the hill. I cradled my rifle and judged, because he was not that far at all, if somebody was to stop walking and take a shot at the base of his neck. at the collar of his jacket, it would be hard to miss even with him on the trot.

I stopped walking. I watched him trotting to the deer, half-giddy like he was.

I raised my gun and I sighted it and I shot him though his collar. He dropped down very quick, quicker than the deer. Like a string holding him up snapped and he dropped to the ground. He rolled and lay on his side, his face half in the snow.

When I got to him his eyes were going already. He looked up at me, breathing a half-buried snort, not confused anymore. I think I made sense to him now. He was fighting for breath, a little. I put my hand on him.

'It's okay,' I said to him. He got his wolf, or his wolf got him, and he was through wondering. I don't know why that was the day, finally. Maybe because I didn't plan to, that day.

It wasn't final, though, because his ghost got right up and got in me. And here I am out here, dying, and I suppose the wolves are going to jump into me, too. Worthless or not, I loved my father. The boy of me did. That died hard, watching his eyes turn grey and his last whiskey-breath come out of him. I loved him, and he did what he did. And I did what I did.

I dragged him through the snow to the river where the deer was drinking before and used his jacket to tie the heaviest stones I could find around him, and dragged him into the water and lay him in a hole in the river I was sure enough wouldn't go dry any time of year. I found more stones to lay on top, and I carried them in too. I left the deer for anybody to find, I didn't want it. I took his rifle home with me. I never reported him missing, and nobody ever missed him, no sheriffs or deputies or police ever came, nobody asked, because he never talked to anybody and neither did I. I walked away from the house soon after, one day, closed the door and never went back.

Out in the world later, I met my wife, and she was every living thing to me. She was life, and my son was, and she saw something in me worth marrying to. I never told her what my father did, or what I did about it.

But bit by bit, those things welled up in me, and bled out of me, and I was no good to her, or our boy.

I asked myself what I could give my son, and the best I could do was ask him to remember always that I loved him, and would always love him. That was a shallow cup to give him. He stared at me and didn't understand what I meant. And I thought the best thing I could give him then was to be far away.

But I prayed he'd remember that I loved him, and that one day it would matter, and he'd believe it at a time it mattered. I tried to tell my wife the same, but she didn't think anything, I suppose, of me telling her I'd always love her. It was no good to her. I looked at her eyes and I saw brightness, even then, I saw my mother who died, the sister she said she'd pretend to be, the daughter I'd never get, and our son, and I went anyway.

There was a day with my father when I was much younger, I got out to the neighbor's, a mile away. He had a dog meaner than anybody, and I was cutting through to get up a hill I liked to get lost on, and the dog got loose and got after me. When my father rambled by in his truck he saw the dog had me in the dirt with its teeth at my neck.

He was out of that truck and on that dog like lightning. He picked it up barking, eighty pounds of pit bull, like it was a puppy. He spun him across the yard yelping and growling, flying, landing on his flank, furious.

He didn't have his gun or anything else, and he got between me and the dog and dared it to come. I think if it came my father would have snapped its neck.

"Get in the truck," he told me, and I ran and got in, and the owner came out. My father told him he'd kill him and his dog if he saw either one of them anywhere near me again. Never mind I was asking for it, cutting through their land. He'd kill them. I watched him, thinking he was going to do it right then.

Whatever happened to my father between that day and the other I don't know. Maybe it happened before I was born, like whatever made me no good to my son happened before I got him. Things get in you that grow later, decide you later. But they were half-decided long ago. Maybe you don't ever know.

It's funny what comes out of you. Get close to your death, you empty yourself out like a bucket. Be empty for the trip. Maybe I want to be empty for the trip.

We're in trees again. The dead wolves are behind us, and there's still light in the sky. I'm confused by the light, because this day should be the shortest, or shorter than the others, it's holding on. We follow a bank of snow through a break in the trees and it

135

drops down steeper, until suddenly we're looking down a chute, a dead stream. Dead trees criss-crossing, some kind of timber-fall.

From where we are it looks to be the only way forward, or the easiest, bad as it looks. I can't seem to get air in my lungs, or in my head. I'm dizzy again, but I don't know what from. My arm bleeding or no food or no sleep, or cold. I can't think of my own name, again, but it isn't lost forever I know. We look down the chute.

I see where it bottoms out there's snow, and there's a cliff edge past it. The snow and the trees drop off and there's nothing past that, just air. I stare at it, figuring the way, through the broken trees, and I think I hear a river again. But it doesn't sound like water running like before, it sounds like wind rumbling, thunder even. I stay still and listen. I still hear it rumbling, under ice maybe but something bigger than the last one is running, down below, off the edge.

I start clambering down through the dead trees, Henrick and Tlingit climbing down behind me. I stumble out of the bottom of it, into a rocky gully buried in snow, and I think what we came down it must have been a waterfall once, or it is in spring.

Down on the snow I can hear water booming now, muffled still, but it's a real river. Henrick and Tlingit make it down through the fall. We go out toward the ledge, toward the sound. It gets louder and louder. Finally we looks down off the edge and see it. We all look down at it.

Even far below us we can see it's big, twice or three times as wide maybe as the one that fooled us before, and deeper, and running like a ribbon of misplaced ocean through the snow, part-frozen but running. It's thundering over the drops, full and fast. Boulders of ice run down it.

"That one might go somewhere," I say.

It's a real river, or feeds one, it must. I'm convincing myself it goes somewhere that isn't here, away from wolves. I don't think it's dead-ending in a lake somewhere. Tlingit laughs.

"Think we can follow that?" Tlingit says.

We all look down the cliff. It's dizzy and jagged. We're standing on an overhang, it looks like. I look to the sides, and I don't even see rock hardly. The face is coated with ice laid on winter after winter, packed snow that must have driven and clung there over the years, a hundred years, or ten-thousand, all the way to the bottom.

I stare down at the river wishing I had more blood in me. It looks beautiful. I look downstream and up to see if there are places the cliff will let us down to the water. It seems to go forever, but I look as far downstream as I can make out, and I think I can see the cliff dropping, hard as it is to make out at that distance in all the white. It looks as if we'll get down to it, if we follow the cliff far enough. It has to drop somewhere. Doesn't matter. What matters is we see it and we can follow it.

We're all so beat and spent but I feel for the first time if I don't bleed out we might get home. I'm confused that there's still daylight but there is, I think this is the last day and it's supposed to be the shortest, but today it seems to have stayed light longer.

But if this is the last of the light now maybe it stayed light so we could find this. Or I'm glad it did, anyway. But finally I see it is starting to fade, but I don't mind, suddenly. The river's so loud I can follow it even if the sun never rises again. I fall back, sitting in the snow.

I look at Henrick and Tlingit. They turn to me, and I find myself smiling at them. They smile, too, and Henrick starts to laugh.

There's a crack. I don't know what it is at first, but Henrick's sliding backwards and then the snow under him and Tlingit just disappears and he and Tlingit drop away from me. I jump for them but I fall, smacking on the snow of the lip, tilting, face-down and feet up but holding on to the snow, my hands dug in, and watching them go, neither of them yelling out, and I see nothing's between them and the bottom, nothing. They aren't going to bounce or have a chance to break the fall or slow down, they are falling through the air away from me, and I'm roaring from my guts and looking at them as they finally start to scream, falling away.

Henrick hits the ice, at the bottom, and then Tlingit right after, two muffled little gunshots, far away. I stare down at them. They didn't smash to pieces. They just landed on the snow near the river. But I see red leaking out around them, like halos.

I keep looking down at them, not so many feet apart from each other but a hundred, maybe two hundred feet below me. They haven't moved, and I know they won't, and there's no going to get them.

I remember Henrick had the wallets, the ones we got, anyway. So they'll be buried there, with them, by the snow, or taken away by the wind, eventually, when his pack rots around him, the wind will find them eventually, leaf through them.

I lie there clinging to the broken edge and being afraid to climb up backwards and afraid what's under me is going to give any minute like it did under them.

I start crawling backward, slowly, up away from the edge, still terrified the snow I'm on is going to slide off with me on it like it's sliding off a roof, but I keep creeping up until I'm far enough back I think I'm on whatever is solid, and then I pull myself up and stumble back from the edge much farther than I need to probably and fall back sitting in the snow, like I was when they dropped away.

I sit there, staring at the empty space off the cliff, I can't see them below anymore, just empty air where the cliff drops away. I stare at it, and I start crying, out of my guts, with anger, because I wanted them to go home, I wanted to get them there. But I know I'm not crying because I wanted them to go home, I'm crying because I want to go home, and I'm alone now, and none of us has made it. I want to go home alive and find my son, whatever I am, however knowing me would ruin him, make him the murderous mess I am, I don't care. I want to guard his life with mine, and guard my wife's, and not leave it to anyone else ever again. I blink, slowly, with cold and blood going away from me. I feel like I'm sinking, falling away, like Henrick and Tlingit fell away from me.

Finally I've been sitting there long enough that the cold is moving up my bones again and I know I have to move. I look at the edge, the empty air. God bless you, I think, looking at them. And then I say it, aloud, on the air.

"God bless you," I say. "Bless you," I say again, louder, for all of us. I know I can sit, and freeze, or wait for the wolves, or admit my chances are used and gone, and that I'll never get home, or I can get up. I feel like I weigh ten thousand pounds. Maybe the time has been determined, anyway, finally.

I get up. I remember what I could see from the edge when I looked downstream. I know the way I want to go. If I can keep the river and get lucky enough to get down to it and get across wherever I can, I know what to do. I can walk home. I can want to, anyway.

I try to see the best way through the trees. I start off, and I find myself calculating how if I could work my way down to the river however any miles ahead I could get back to Henrick and Tlingit's bodies, to do what, I don't know. See if they lived through it. Say goodbye, cover them in snow. Get their wallets, and the others Henrick had. Which are all stupid thoughts. I think them, anyway.

12

HEADING DOWN THE slope I know I'm not walking even as well as before. I look at my arm again. Blood's still crusted but the skin under it looks white. I don't know if it's that's the bandage wrapped too tight or if my hand is just dying. I wonder if it can start in your hand and spread to the rest of you. That would have started in my head if that were true.

I stop and look back at all the country behind me, where Henrick and Tlingit and all the others are lying dead, and behind them, the plane and its dead are probably covered in snow.

I walk on as the light fades again. I try to mark things I might know in the dark that's about to fall. The trees open to a little clearing, ringed by rocks and another little bluff going up away from the cliff-edge. I look down to the edge again, and I realize the river's louder now. It makes me think the cliffs are lower.

I go to the edge to see how low. I feel a cool push of air up from the freezing water. It feels wet, the air, or I think it does. Sure enough the cliff isn't as high above as it was. It's dropping, not a lot but it is. I look to what's ahead of me, where I have to pick my way.

I try to see my way through, and ahead, among the trees and rocks and snow, I see the wolves are there. But then I see it's only the big one. I thought I saw others with him but they were only rocks or shadows or branches. It's just the one, up on a hump of snow, between trees. The others gave up maybe or died, or sat down in the snow and didn't want to get up again.

He's looking down at me, like the rocks are looking. Like the trees are, and the sky is, patiently, not angry in particular that I can see. Just looking. And the wind moves, and that's him thinking about me, I think. If he thinks of me, it's no more than that. Air moving through trees.

There's enough light left I can still see where he's cut, bloody in places. His wounds look worse than before. I realize why it's a long time since I saw him, he's been distracted by dying.

Seeing him now I know that to think I would have made it down to the river, or made it home, was something I was dreaming.

I stare at him a long time before I do anything else. I'm tired. I suppose we aren't going to nod to each other and let each other go our ways, to die on our own, somewhere.

I fumble my knife out of my pocket. It falls through my fingers to the snow and I look up at him. He steps down a little. He's slowing, like me. The light's going though, and my eyes are. I don't know what I'm seeing. Light's going from my head, too. I'm not all the way sure of anything. He shows his teeth, comes closer.

I blink, suck air in. I don't want to do whatever it is I'll have to do to live this out. Maybe I've been dead for a day anyway, maybe the blood I lost at the plane. Maybe it was decided a night and a day ago. Or much longer ago.

There are blurs. He launches up at me. I know there won't be any fighting this. I'm dying now, finally, in blurs. I'm punching at wherever pain is. The light's dropping away and I'm going to die at last light. I think I may be dying. Things are starting to go away to where they've been going since I got here.

He's still pulling at me and I think I'm fighting, I don't know, I don't know how many I'm fighting. I think only the last one. I feel him slacken, but I think I'm falling over. I fall to the snow with him, and somehow get up, and he's flopping his paws in the snow, weakly.

I'm bleeding more now from new places. It's a lot of blood and I'm blurring, more, and colder. I'm disappearing, dreaming on my feet. It gets darker. My eyes go darker from the edges in, like the night has crawled up from the snow and air and is seeping into me. Shreds of light are in the sky, swallowed by dark.

I blink, trying to keep seeing. I don't know if I 'm standing or not or if my eyes are open or not, and I twitch my hand to tell if my knife is there or still in the snow. I look, in my dream, to see if the big wolf is getting up and coming. But in my dream he's still standing on the rise above me looking down, or he's trotted up there, in front of me, up on his paws again.

I think of my wife and my son, and I think I was a man once, far away I was a man, in the world, and I remembered my name. I was not a dream floating into grey.

There's nothing in me but the last things, my wife as she was, my son when he was mine.

I look at my wolf. If you're my death, I think, if you're all the wrongs I've done, none of the things I am and none of the things I've done will touch my wife, or my son. I'll end here, forever.

I look at him, I dream, and he looks like death again. He leaps into the air and I think I fall again. I hit the snow and I don't try to move. There's nothing of me, and I see the last shred of light in the sky go out. I'm swimming in the snow in dark, dreaming I'm standing over him, and all the others are dead in the snow and standing around me at the same time.

I dream I hoist him on my shoulders, because seeing him in the snow, breathing out last breaths, is too much to bear. I lift him and wrap him in magic blankets, under the sky.

I carry him with me, and I am sliding off the edge of the cliff where Tlingit and Henrick went, slipping over after them, looking down. The wallets are open to the wind, blowing. Henrick is worn to bones.

The wind has gotten in and taken the wallets and all that's in them to itself, blowing them away, like me, blowing down to the river, carrying my wolf, and all my wolves, through the dark to the cold water and rocks and ice.

I fall and fall, something floats away and I don't feel anything but cold dark, turning over, drifting, down a river over rocks and mud and ice, tumbling over and under me, rushing and thundering and flowing through life and death and heaven.

I'm fighting him, or I've fought him, and I think a last thing, quite peacefully, I think goodbye, and I am nearly gone, then gone, sleep in sleep and dark in dark.

I'm standing in the motel, at the door, staring at the picture I left on the nightstand. I'm closing the door on it. I'm a hundred yards up the hall, a thousand, ten thousand. I'm standing there, stopped, a mortal fool. I'm back in the room again, stuffing the picture back into my wallet, my wife, smiling, my son, laughing. I'm taking them with me, I think.

I'm dreaming, somewhere on the snow, near the plane, and the picture that's all that's left of me is blowing, tumbling over snow past the pieces of plane, through the dead and the cold, far from the world, lifting into air. I am blowing away with it toward all that's gone from me. There's moonlight, I think, or the sun but there's no more sun.

But there's water pounding, thundering, I'm half drowning, freezing in mud. There are magic wolves and a magic river and magic blankets, floating and lighting in the sky like aurora.

I dream lights and ropes and people are coming to take me to my wife again, and my boy again, around the curve of the earth, and I'm praying, and I see the lights are aurora. Green-gold, purple. I realize, finally, that they're souls, lighting the sky and dancing. Anybody can see that, it should be obvious to anyone. I close my eyes, and open them again.

There is aurora again, dancing, like the night in the snow. There's a hand, reaching down, telling me I can go home to my wife, and home to my son.

In my dream, I take the hand.

CPSIA information can be obtained at www.ICGtesting.com
Printed in the USA
LVOW11s1940160614

390268LV00001B/101/P